Kentucky Rain

This book is a work of fiction. Names, characters, and incidents are either the product of the author's imagination or are used fictitiously, and any resemblance to actual persons, living or dead, events, or their outcomes is entirely coincidental.

To order additional copies, please contact us.
BookSurge, LLC
www.booksurge.com
1-866-308-6235
orders@booksurge.com

CHARLOTTE
JERACE

KENTUCKY RAIN

A Novel

2006

Kentucky Rain

Strength and dignity are her clothing;
And she laugheth at the time to come.
She openeth her mouth with wisdom
And the law of kindness is on her tongue.

Proverbs

ACKNOWLEDGEMENTS

Throughout the daunting effort of writing *Kentucky Rain*, I have been blessed to have the unyielding support and encouragement of Andrea Asimow. With her critical eye and gentle words, Andrea has challenged me to peel back the layers of my characters and helped me to understand better how to tell a story. Andrea, I am honored.

As always, I am grateful to my family for their love and understanding.

CJ
Truro, Massachusetts
4 October 2006

For Mary and Michael

PRINCE EDWARD ISLAND, CANADA

"I'm exhausted. I've been on four airplanes since I left home. I need a cocktail and this man is pawing through my bloomers. Who does he think he is anyway, Sgt. Presley of the Yukon with his dog, King? He reminds me of one of my old bones that I met under the clock at the Biltmore, stiff with no sense of humor. I just don't understand why he's mad that I didn't tell him that I have a bottle of bourbon in my valise? It's not new; you can see that it's used. They need to learn to mind their manners in Canada. It's nobody's business what I choose to bring into their country. After all, I'm their guest, aren't I? Well, I've lost my patience. There's only one thing to do when a boy bullies a girl. Haul off and smack him!"

"The party waiting for Agatha Rose Vorelli should come to Customs and Immigration immediately."

Although I've lived in Canada for twenty years, a small chill passes over me. It sounds so legal and troublesome. On the other hand, I'm relieved. Thank God, she's finally here.

"She's probably tried to sneak in something without declaring it," I say hopefully as we hurry to the other end of the airport. My husband nods knowingly, grateful that our drama is ending.

The Mountie is a rookie, lives by the book, and stands straight as a steel rod. He leads us to the "detained visitor" who is delighted to see us. She offers a gentle hug to me, a bigger one to Mac, and then starts to close her suitcase.

"Not yet, Ma'am," the Mountie warns. He's very serious, not cracking a smile, impatient to wrap this up.

"Young man," Mom says, with the same tone she used to use when Paul had done something wrong. "I've had it with you." She slams her suitcase shut and then sticks out her tongue at him. It is at this moment that I notice she is wearing barrettes in her hair. Not the fashionable tortoise-shell kind, her's are little girl barrettes, pink, yellow and white, all shaped like teddy bears. As I stand there slack-jawed, she removes one of her barrettes, turns it into a weapon, and proceeds to snip at the Mountie.

"Agatha Rose, now stop that," Mac says laughing nervously.

Mom turns to Mac, sticks out her tongue and pouts.

"Ma'am, if you don't behave I am going to charge you

with smuggling and assault!" Mom laughs while I gasp and Mac tries the diplomatic approach.

"Look, she's missed three planes, she's exhausted and this is highly unusual behavior. My wife's been hysterical on the phone with her sister and brother in the States, and the whole family is going crazy with worry. We would appreciate it if you'll just let us get her to our home."

The Mountie shifts his weight from side to side, clearly in a quandary.

Mac lowers his voice, looks him straight in the eye. "Give us a break, eh? What would you do if this was your mother?"

The Mountie gives my mother another stern look." Follow me," he says, escorting us to the terminal door, which he holds open for us to pass.

"We're very grateful," I want to say more but Mom is pushing my shoulder.

"Take care of her," he says.

"Thanks, we'll do that." Mac carries her suitcase while I take her hand and hurry off to our car.

Mom stops to gaze at the stars. One of the many good things about living on our island is the lack of illumination from city lights. On clear nights, the stars and planets twinkle brilliantly against an inky sky. Tonight is no exception.

Mom squints until she spots the Big Dipper. She waves at it, and then looks at me quizzically. "Darling, what are you doing here?"

"What do you mean, Mom?"

"You shouldn't have driven all the way to Halifax; I would have flown to Charlottetown!"

"Mom, you *did* fly to Charlottetown." What's wrong with her?

A blank stare, then, "How nice." Another blank look then

she says, "You really shouldn't have come all this way, I could have flown the rest of the way."

Our conversation is repeated all the way home and if that isn't enough, Mom's suit is covered with cat hair. She isn't in the car for five minutes before Mac begins wheezing, his eyes tearing and swelling simultaneously. Luckily, he finds some Benadryl in the glove box that he swigs down with cold coffee. The moment we get home, he takes three allergy pills, and then conks out in his Barcolounger.

Mom seems genuinely glad to be in our home. Rather, Mom seems glad to be in a place where she can get a fresh drink. It's late, she's tired, and so I decide to water it down. I try to ignore my racing heart and the burning pit in my stomach. Something is very wrong with my mother.

Just as I'm about to burst into tears, I see her walking around my living room. Her posture is graceful and erect as she studies Mac's paintings and my woven tapestries that dress the walls. From her bearing you'd swear it was dear old Mom, the social butterfly, debutante, Vassar grad, just making the rounds of her hostess' home.

"Are you joining me?" she trills, taking her favorite chair as I hand her the glass.

"Just let me get the pate and Brie so we can nibble while dinner heats up."

Mom settles back, smiles warmly, takes a dainty sip, offers a big grin, and then sighs.

I return with the hors d'ouevres and place the tray in front of her. It's the good delft tray that she'd brought to us as a housewarming gift when we put on the addition five years ago. She smiles as she recognizes the tray, which makes me happy until her smile becomes a frown.

"What's wrong?" My eyelids begin to twitch.

She shakes her head. "I've been looking for that tray for years. Why would you do such a thing?" She squares her shoulders and blinks furiously.

The burning pit in my stomach fires up again. "Do what?" I manage to ask.

Her blue eyes bore into mine. "Steal it."

The hair on the back of my neck springs up. "You gave this tray to Mac and me when we built the addition," I flare. Then, as I stand there ready to do battle with my mother, her expression softens. She spreads a water cracker with a dainty dab of pate, takes a finishing school nibble, and then smiles angelically. "Delicious, dear. Is that bourbon you've added, or Grand Marnier?"

I can barely answer.

All is forgotten and we manage beautifully through dinner. I've made salmon croquettes, one of her favorite dishes, and she is genuinely pleased at my effort. I've taken care to stock up and plan for all of her favorite meals.

"Exquisite," she says after each bite.

"You taught her well, Aggie Ro," Mac says, guzzling coffee in a losing fight with Benadryl's groggy effect.

"Oh, she's a talent, that one," Mom raises her glass in my direction.

I try to relax. When we finish, I offer decaf.

"No thank you, dear, I'd like a shit of brandy before I go night-night."

"A what?"

"A sip of brandy, Soph. I'll get it." Mac rescues her, leaving me alarmed. She's either losing her mind or she's tipsy from the watered-down drink. Let it be the latter, I pray.

After settling her into bed, I check the answering machine. I have a total of eight messages: four from Paul, two from Izzy, and two from Air Canada. I call Paul and he conferences in my sister.

"All she had to do was fly from Madison to Montreal, change in Montreal to fly to Halifax, then change again to fly to Charlottetown. She was due to arrive at 1:05. Where in hell was she until 7:20 pm?"

"She said that she had to wait a long time in what she thought was Chicago, but she's unsure. She said lots of people came and went on different planes, but her flight was never called."

"What time did you start calling Air Canada?" Paul speaks as if he is taking notes for a lawsuit.

"It doesn't matter, bro. Eventually, someone must have noticed her. Mom says a very nice woman in a navy blue suit put her on a tiny little plane filled with men wearing pretty sweaters and pastel trousers."

"I love it," Izzy laughs.

"She did, too. She couldn't stop giggling when she announced that she was the only girl. Mac figures that it was the golfers special. They get a real deal for traipsing around in the mud off-season."

"We need to find out what happened," he insists.

"Be my guest." I have lots to do now that she's here and frankly I think Air Canada has heard enough from me for awhile.

TWO

A fter settling Mom in our guest room, I climb the stairs and flop down next to Mac. Even though I am desperate to speak with him, I don't have the heart to wake him. Instead, I think about Mom.

She's been coming to the Island ever since I moved here. In fact, for a time she talked about making the Island her home. She's part Scottish, loves the fact that there are a ton of Scots who've settled here. When she comes up, we go to Highland Games, listen to the bagpipers, eat haggis, shop for tartans and read period novels aloud to each other. Usually, she comes twice a year, once in the winter if I haven't been home for Christmas, and once in the summer. This year, I couldn't get there at Christmas because I have a pastry-baking business I run from my home. I was so swamped with orders up until the last minute that I couldn't imagine finding the strength to get home.

It was Paul who came up with an alternative. Mom would fly up here to visit for a few weeks, and then I'd drive with her to Louisville, Kentucky in time for the May running of the Kentucky Derby. She's been under the weather, the break would work wonders, and I'd get a whole month with my mom. It's a great idea because I've been a worried about her. She's been stumbling with her words on the phone, has stopped writing long letters and she's had a car accident. This visit will give me time to figure out what's going on.

THREE

Mom finally awakens after sleeping nine hours. She takes two hours to eat breakfast and then decides to get dressed. Together, we open her suitcase and at first it looks like someone has played a joke on her. But that someone is my mother.

Incredibly, she has not packed anything practical, no slacks or sweaters, but she did bring twenty-three pairs of panties! My slim, trim mother also brought a long-line girdle, although it appears to never have been worn. She has also packed a half-dozen wrist-length and full-length pairs of kid gloves in assorted shades.

"What are you planning to wear today?" I ask, while putting her things in the drawer I've emptied for her.

"Ta dah!" She smiles that impish grin, holds up her long royal blue velvet skirt and a Cape Cod sweatshirt. I remain speechless.

She *has* brought one blouse with a lovely dark stain on it. Stuffed in an ancient Bonwit Teller bag are her three-inch alligator high-heels and the silver high-heeled sandals she wore when she danced with Charleton Heston while he was in Madrid filming *El Cid*. Fortunately, she wore her loafers on the plane.

Digging deeper, I find half a box of Oreos, the two bottles of Jim Beam that the Mountie let her keep, Grand-Dahlia's pearls, and an array of ancient makeup and toiletries that boggles the mind. An old Bergdorf's garment bag reveals her beautiful brocade strapless gown with the long flowing scarf that she had made in Spain. Judging by the things she brought, she's planning on a night on the town, probably thinking only of Prince Edward and forgetting the "Island". Anyway, just as I'm giving up hope for anything that makes sense, there, at the bottom of her suitcase is her hyacinth blue suit, with her sapphire and diamond pin already in place. She'll wear it to the Derby, of course.

"I'd like to shop for a new cat," she announces. It takes me a full minute before I realize that she means "hat" and that is only the beginning of what I'm dealing with. I realize now how much *we all* are in denial, or just unaware of her situation. It dawns on me that our trip to Kentucky will be a much larger task than I am prepared for!

As far as the packing goes, the items she forgot are all things that are relatively easy to replace or make do without, but the big issue is that she has brought the WRONG BOOK.

"Why would the Louisville Historical Society want a book on the Alhambra?" I ask, feeling my skin prickle.

She stares at me as if I were a Martian. "I don't know, dear. Why would they?" Mom knows that she's brought a book to take to Louisville Historical Society, but doesn't really grasp that it's the wrong one until we open it and she doesn't see any family photos.

"Call Nelly, and ask her to ship it up here," Mac suggests. Why didn't I think of that? Mom's neighbor and closest friend answers on the first ring, happy to hear that Mom has arrived safe and sound and that I have her "under my wing". She'll just let herself in to Mom's house and call right back.

I spend a good five minutes on the phone with Nelly describing the unique book. "It's dark brown, with no writing on the spine, but the cover says 'Louisville'. A hand-written journal has been bound inside, along with lots of photographs. It's priceless, Nelly, the only one in existence."

Hours later, Nelly delivers the bad news.

"Let me be delicate, dear." Nelly clears her throat several times before she spells it out.

"Mother's housekeeping isn't what it used to be." Damn. This is the gossipy Nelly that we've all learned to watch out for.

"I know. But did you find it?"

"No. I can't find it anywhere, Sophia. Maybe she took it to the library."

Oh my God. In her confused state what if she did just that? With my heart sinking slowly I call the library and try to be patient while the librarian checks the stacks. After a good fifteen minutes, I hear the clop clop of her footsteps against the polished floors I remember so well. They grow louder until she reaches her desk.

"Sorry, it's not here," she says in her flat Midwestern accent.

I don't know if I'm relieved or worried, but this really puts a kink in our plans. I can't see any other alternative but to go to Wisconsin and get the damn book. It is, after all, one of the two major reasons for this trip to Louisville. Dammit. We'll have to allow an extra week or two for the detour!

I start slamming drawers until Mac comes in, slides his rough, warm hand over mine. "What's up, Chiquita?" he uses his sexy voice, somewhat out of place for the occasion.

When I tell him, he swallows hard; the muscle near his jaw twitches his concern.

"I only have two weeks off, baby. You're looking at a three week trip." He rubs my shoulders, now taut and painful, as I realize what's ahead.

"I've got to get to my meeting." I'm trembling as I race out the door.

FOUR

A dozen or more cars fill the parking lot at the senior center. I'm glad for the small turnout, because tonight I need to speak.

"Hi, I'm Sophia and I'm an alcoholic."

"Hi, Sophia," the group answers and the room grows warmer.

"I've been sober for two years now but this is the first time I've been sober around my mother for an extended period of time. She might have Alzheimer's and we are going to take a road trip together and she drinks," I blurt. A murmur sweeps through the room.

"My siblings are no help...one is a workaholic, the other a druggie, although neither admits it. Besides, I'm the one who always steps up to the plate and that's fine, except this time things aren't normal. It would be funny. I mean, I could make you wet your pants if it wasn't so sad."

Someone says, "Your sobriety is the most important thing in your life." AA speak, smart, for sure, but we're talking about my mother. She's the woman in the red crewneck sweater and plaid blouse, a pair of pressed chinos and penny loafers, who cheered me on when I ran across a soccer field, then kissed my scraped knees and treated me to homemade apple pie, win or lose. She's the one who took care of *me*. After the accident she never left my side.

I get what I need from the meeting—affirmation, support. After a few hugs and a Betty Crocker brownie, I'm out the door, driving under a blanket of stars to Mom, Mac and impending madness.

Mac suggests that I call Paul to see if maybe he could meet me halfway to share the driving. It's a mistake. He is in such denial that he can't imagine the state Mom is in even when I tell him that last night I heard her walking around in her room repeating over and over, "I want to go home, I just want to go home."

Instead of showing a little understanding, Paul is tense. He clips his words, sending a chill through the telephone lines.

"Why do I feel like I'm about to be attacked?" I ask, as goose bumps rise.

He whistles, sighs, and then springs. "These phone calls about our mother being demented are very distracting, Soph, especially, when they are so far-fetched."

"You just can't face the truth, Paul." I want to say more but he cuts me off.

"Listen to me. I blew it in court today, big time. I never should have taken your call knowing that I had to argue in front of Shirley McGee, the toughest judge on the circuit, a real ball breaker.

I want to laugh. It's my fault that the big Boston lawyer blew it. "Sorry, but I'd say this is pretty important, Paul."

Paul has always been wrapped up in his own world and today is no exception. "I walked into Court and first off the bailiff whispers to me that my fly is unzipped. Next, I opened my briefcase, and dammit, it was Alicia's briefcase. So I reached for my cell phone and realized that I left it in the car. Then I ran to the pay phone to call the house and couldn't remember my own phone number.

"Maybe I'm dense, but what does this have to do with Mom?" I ask, trying to ignore the heat rising in my face.

He yells, "Are you that thick? Does this mean I have dementia or Alzheimer's? No, it means that I am so nervous about the damn case that I was driven to distraction. Plus, my phone numbers are all programmed so I can just push a button. Christ, with all these pin numbers to remember we're all going nuts. So what if Mom packed weirdly and brought the wrong book?"

"Paul." I brace myself, can feel it coming.

"It gets worse. The friggin' judge caught me staring off into space for a minute, so she smashed her gavel against the microphone to be sure everyone else saw it too. And I have you to thank, Sophia, because of your need to give me a blow by blow exaggerated report about Mom."

"You're unbelievable!" The back of my head prickles.

"How articulate! You think you can just lay this Mom stuff on me and that I don't react? I walked into court, sat down, ready to earn my living when somewhere in the back of my head I heard Mom's voice." He pauses, and then softly repeats the poem that she said only to him. "One potato, two potatoes, three potatoes, four, Paul is the sweetest boy that I adore…"

My eyes well up. He's still Mom's baby boy. "You think I don't understand? I have this in front of my face! The point is that we've all been in denial," I say gingerly. There is silence until he erupts.

"Next time you start to fantasize that she has Alzheimer's, make yourself a toddy and climb under a rock."

Slam. Breathe slowly, I tell myself.

Paul calls right back. "I take back the toddy remark, kid."

"Screw you."

His voice is softer now. "Just because she's forgetful doesn't mean she has Alzheimer's, Soph. We need to get her to a doctor, have her evaluated and then we can react.

"Fine."

"If I could fly to PEI I would, but the case is at a sensitive point and if I leave now I could jeopardize the outcome."

"She isn't connecting the dots, bro".

He groans. It's dismissive, or so I think. Instead, he surprises me. "I'll call Izzy and conference her in later, maybe nine your time."

Okey dokey. I can't wait for the call.

Meanwhile, I call Chief Halvorsen in Belle Haven to get the real details on her accident.

I give my siblings a full report. Of course I'm a little aggravated that my brother, the lawyer, hadn't checked this out previously, but okay, he's working on the "big" case he's waited for his whole career. He says, "This is the big enchilada, baby."

I check the notes I made when I spoke with the Chief.

"The accident itself wasn't serious, thank God, and you have to chuckle a little. Mom had stopped for a family of ducks to cross the road."

"Naturally," Izzy laughs.

"Apparently she really slammed on the brakes. Chief Halvorsen said that the guy who rear-ended her was really pissed when she drove off and never looked back. When the chief sent some cops to the house to investigate, she wouldn't let them in. She yelled at them through the door that the gas pedal just got stuck and wouldn't let up until she got home! She never bothered to explain why she ditched her car a block from the house."

"Jesus," says Paul.

"Hmmm," Izzy hums.

Now I get up my nerve. "Chief Halvorsen feels it's time to stop her from driving."

"Christ," says Paul. "Izzy, what do you think?"

"A rear-ender? This is a reason to take her license away and sell her car? In LA people drive stoned, or they can't even read the signs. I say we all chill."

"Isabela," I'm about to argue, but she interrupts.

"Like really chill out, Sophia. If you could hear yourself when you talk to us you'd know you're in your manic panic mode. There are some great meds like Topomax or Tegretol, but probably National Health won't pay for things like that."

Slam, dunk, score Isabela bitch. "No, we are not financially secure. Yes, Mac and I have to stretch to make ends meet at the end of the month. And yes, National Health is strict on what they'll pay for, but at least the meds I take are prescribed!"

"Girls!"

"Listen Paul, I don't need this right now."

"I'm sure you don't, but I'm in Boston and Izzy's in LA. It's hard to know how serious this is."

"It's serious, you can count on it."

I hear a clatter out in the yard so I move to the window. It's just the wind blowing over an empty birdseed can; still, it's a good excuse to get off the phone with these two imbeciles.

I walk outside to retrieve the cover before it blows away. The can is almost empty so I take a moment to scatter seeds on top of the remaining snow. I need time to process what's going on in my family.

Paul calls right back.

"You okay?" he asks.

"No. You guys are freaking me out. I don't need her laid back California bullshit. Just so you know, she called me a few weeks ago and she was either smashed or stoned and kept repeating herself. Then she told me she's met someone who looks a lot like Jack!"

"Christ," Paul says.

"I just can't deal with her now. I have an order for a very expensive wedding cake and reception pastries—enough profit to cover most of the meals on the trip with Mom."

"I'm glad your business is taking off, Sis." I know he means it. My financial security has always been something he worries about.

"It's hard work, but I love it. And I'm making little doggies out of Marzipan. Can you imagine anything more delectable?"

"Send me a picture. It sounds spectacular!"

"Okay, gotta go."

"Love you, Soph."

"Love you, too."

"And Soph, she didn't mean to hurt you by mentioning Jack. Cut her some slack."

"Okay," I grumble. But it's not okay. Jack has been missing from our lives for thirty years.

FIVE

Thirty years can seem like a lifetime, but when it comes to remembering Jack, the years fall away and he slips out of the shadows.

Jack Thibodeau had been Mac's roommate for their sophomore and junior years at the University of Michigan. He was a varsity hockey player, fearless on the ice, using speed, agility and masterful puck handling to lead his team to the league championship. The son of a French Canadian lumberjack and a soft-spoken pastry chef, Jack started college knowing that he'd have to hold down two jobs to supplement his athletic scholarship.

They were quite a pair. As attractive as Mac is with his dark good looks and rock-hard body, Jack was the type of guy whose looks grew on you. His face was meaty and scarred from hockey mishaps; still it pulled you in like a magnet. I used to describe Jack as rugged, like a big, brown bear. He carried a little paunch thanks to a voracious appetite, but it just made him more endearing. The frosting on the cake was his smile, flashing white chicklets, with a half-inch gap separating his two front teeth. His smile was so disarming, that even if you didn't know him, you just had to smile back.

As if being a hockey star wasn't enough to make him one of the most popular men on the huge Michigan campus, he was better known for his impersonation of Elvis Presley. Jack could drawl and swivel his hips sounding just like the King—albeit with a tinge of French Canadian peppering his fake Southern account. As word of Jack's "other" talent spread, it eventually spilled onto the hockey rink. Whenever he slap-sticked a goal, the crowd would chant, "Elvis, Elvis," much to the confusion of the opposing team.

By the middle of their junior year, Mac became Jack's "manager" and took to wearing Colonel Tom Parker's big Stetson hat around campus. He even chomped on an unlit cigar to round out the image. Needless to say, Mac and Jack became famous throughout Ann Arbor. Within a few short weeks of launching their partnership, Mac was so successful in arranging gigs, Jack was able to quit his other two jobs.

When the real Elvis performed at the Olympia Stadium in Detroit in October, 1974, Mac scored two of the best seats in the house. My girlfriends and I were at the concert, too, although I don't remember seeing Mac and Jack. Like everyone, my eyes were fastened on Elvis, mesmerized by his still-handsome face, while trying to ignore his surprising paunch and too thick sideburns. It was the beginning of Elvis' downward spiral, but I didn't know it then. What I did know is that when he sang "Burning Love" and curled his lip, I felt heat fire up my mid-section. I still can't believe he's gone.

The following semester, Mac and Jack and I formed a friendship when we were seated next to each other in a creative writing class. We admired each other's stories, shared the same dry sense of humor and, of course, were linked in our love for Elvis Presley. I can't remember if it was Mac or Jack that invited me to hang out with them, but it wasn't long before I was cheering the guys at their hockey games and they were taking me along to their gigs. After a concert, they always asked for my opinion. When I volunteered to use my sewing skills to embroider Jack's jumpsuit and cape, I became the official wardrobe mistress. My favorite part of the job was standing in the wings to hand Jack some cheap scarves that he could distribute to his adoring fans—just like The King did. To this day I wish I had saved just one of those scarves. Just one.

During short school breaks, I would invite Jack to my home in Wisconsin. It was expensive to travel back east, plus we enjoyed being able to kick back and just hang out without the pressure of school. Mac, who had more spending money, would sometimes meet up with his girlfriend at her aunt's house in New York. Other times, he'd come along to Belle Haven.

The Vorellis became Jack's extended family as naturally as if he had grown up next door. If paint needed to be scraped, Jack was first with the putty knife. When the pressure cooker exploded on the stove, Jack sat Mom down and cleaned up the mess. Paul loved shooting hoops with Jack, who was smart enough to let him win occasionally. Even Izzy, ever the rebel, was enchanted with my buddy. Izzy would pester him to dance with her, oblivious that despite the great Elvis imitations, Jack had two left feet. The only dance he could do well was the Twist, which he taught Izzy to do so well that she won a dance contest later in the year. Quite simply, she adored him. She mimicked his Canuck accent relentlessly and he would play along. His favorite line was, "I come down on my bicycle, me." No matter how many times he said it, Mom and Izzy would break into peels of laughter. Then Jack would put straws up his nostrils and twirl them with his tongue until Mom and Izzy ran away, clutching their stomachs, and my weak bladder betrayed me.

Jack became Paul's idol. He would spend hours with my little brother, teaching him to play the guitar, sing like the King, and to curl his lip. Eventually, Paul could even swivel his hips. My father would stand in the doorway in mock horror, teasing them by singing opera every time they took a break, but Mom loved every second of it. She swooned at the curled lips and moving hips, pretending to faint when Jack winked at her.

It got to a point where Paul spent more time with Jack than I did. But I didn't care. After all, Jack was my good buddy, not a boyfriend that I wanted to slip off and neck with.

Early in our friendship, Jack dated one of my roommates for a few months. I'd hang out with him in the lobby waiting for Christy to get ready for their date. Later, I realized that we were always disappointed to stop our conversation when Christy showed up. Jack and I could talk a blue streak about everything and anything, that's how it was with us. Mac was going steady with a girl back home in Maine whom he called every weekend, but rarely saw. He pulled her photograph out of his wallet one time after I suggested that she must be buck-toothed and cross-eyed since no one had ever met her. It turned out that she was drop-dead gorgeous, a dimpled, honey-blonde with a great smile and perfect figure.

On weekends, I usually had a date, flipping between hockey players and nerds, but never found anyone I wanted to spend more than an evening with. It was much more fun being with Mac and Jack.

With the Vietnam war finally over and the Women's Movement in full swing, the mid-seventies were good years for us. I marched in demonstrations a few times and quoted

Gloria Steinem until Mac and Jack begged me to stop. I went braless until I realized that my runaway bosom was attracting the kind of attention I did not want. With doors opening for women everywhere, I saw a future filled with promise. I wanted to be a journalist, and I was able to publish a few articles in the school newspaper. But most of all, I wanted to be somewhere close to Jack and Mac—in that order.

We decided that after graduation we would wait and see who landed the first job, and that would be where we'd all live. It was a promise we meant to keep.

SIX

Today, Mom appears to have recuperated from her ordeal getting out here, but she's quite confused. I'm beginning to realize that this is not likely to go away. Mac says that she'd probably be more comfortable and less confused in the familiar surroundings of her own home. Even with her situation, she is really no trouble, content to sit and work on a crossword puzzle, which takes her all day instead of the few minutes it used to. She only reads the front page of the newspaper now, though she finds it very funny and shares it out loud with me, many, many times over. I must admit that my humor wears thin but at least she's enjoying it. I'm so glad that we aren't putting off our trip to Kentucky for another year as we had discussed. I just hope she'll know she's there!

After lunch and her nap, I pull out the Scrabble game. Mom and Papa loved to spar over scrabble. They had their own rules; played with fourteen letters instead of seven. She was a pro at making up words and convincing Papa that they were real. "It's because you speak English as a second language that you haven't heard of it," she'd say. My favorite time was when she put out the letters H-E-R-M-E-N-E-U-T-I-C-S. "Hermeneutics, triple word, double letters". Papa argued, "That's not a word". The good-natured shouting began until he demanded that Mom explain what the word meant. She could barely keep a straight face as she answered, "Hermeneutics is the study of Hermans".

I set up the board; she counts out seven letters just fine. She begins. She places b-o-t and says "boat".

"No, Mom, boat is spelled b-o-a-t.

"It is not! You are such a know-it-all, Sophia. I'm not playing with you."

She dumps her tiles onto the carpet, jumps out of her chair and storms off indignantly, while I sit here stinging from her words.

SEVEN

The sound of rain pounding on the windowpanes awakens me. I slide out of bed and walk to the landing at the top of the stairs where French doors lead to a small balcony. I'm drawn to the fresh rain like a moth to a flame. In my thin, cotton nightgown I stand on the balcony letting the rain wash over me. I throw my head back, open my mouth and catch raindrops with my tongue until I'm nearly blue with cold. Then I run inside and turn the faucets of the shower on full blast for a hot, steaming shower.

I've always done some of my best thinking surrounded by water. This morning is no exception. As the pulsing water stings my back I analyze Mom's behavior and compare it to what I know about Alzheimer's. The signals are there, staring me in the face. It's the beginning of the end for my mother. The realization hits me like a ton of bricks. Several minutes later Mac finds me curled into a ball in the corner of the shower, my face red from crying.

"I can't believe that this is happening to my mother."

"Yeah, well, no one wants to believe this type of thing," he says toweling me dry.

"What are we going to do?"

"Damned if I know," he says, scratching his head. "Let's have some coffee and talk about it."

"I don't want to."

"I know," he says, planting a kiss on my damp forehead.

Mom asks frequently when we are going to take the book to Kentucky, so at least I know that it's still important to her. The shocker is that she's forgotten what the book is about! Today, I tell her no less than *seven* times. Just when I thought I'd go mad, Kathleen Craig arrives with sugar-free scones to go with a cup of tea and a visit with Mom. Kath has always been one of Mom's favorites and vice versa. I leave them chatting in the kitchen so I can straighten up Mom's room and throw a load of laundry in the machine.

When I return, there's Mom, speaking clearly and in her way, explaining to Kath, "The boot is a history of Louisville. My great-great-grandfather was one of the seven founders of Louisville and his son was the first white male born in Kentucky!

"You don't say." Kath smiles at me.

"Oh but I *do* say," Mom continues. "I own the only copy of this rare boot. They're planning a dinner in my honor, when I give them the..." She stares blankly, having forgotten the word. "Then my mother and I are going to the Derby."

From out of Mom's line of sight I signal Kath that Mom's confused.

Ignoring me, Kath eggs her on. "How much are you going to bet?"

"Oh, fifty cents. I'm really going for the mint juleps." She straightens her back, offers up a smile, and then she's distracted.

Mom turns to me, "Tell her about your Grand-Dahlia, darlin'". So there I am trying not to bore poor Kath with a story about our family, but Mom is listening as if she's a little kid, hearing her favorite story told and retold. She won't let me be short and sweet. I begin with the genealogy thinking that will suffice.

"More, tell it ALL," Mom demands. I shrug my shoulders; it's going to be a long afternoon.

"My grandmother demanded that we kids call her Grand-Dahlia," I say, as my cheeks flush. I'm embarrassed; sitting in my simple kitchen with a plain-living woman whose life mirrors mine. 'Grand-Dahlia' sounds so ostentatious. Still, Mom is impatient for the story. She can't wait to add, "She was a Southern belle". God, how I hate that expression.

"Yeah," I say, "right out of Tennessee Williams, dotty old aunts and all."

With a toss of her head, Mom dismisses my comment, and then gives me "the stare". It's the same look that she gave me when once, during a tough period in my teens, I sassed her in public. Her eyes always held such tremendous power, those startling cornflower blue marbles that drill into your mind without mercy. Today her gaze is steady, but not as strong.

"Tell her about Daddy," she insists and I'm even more uncomfortable, showing off our fancy background.

"Why not?" Kath says as I crunch up my nose. I really don't want to do this.

"Tell her now," Mom raises her voice, squeezes my hand and the two golf-ball sized diamonds set in one magnificent platinum setting, which she inherited from Grand-Dahlia, flash from her slender, blue-veined finger. So I say, "Grandpa was from the North."

"A Yankee!" she hoots and laughs, then leans forward, eyes dancing, loving the story. She taps her hand twice, impatient to hear the whole nine yards.

I speak faster, and then roll my eyes apologetically to Kath. "He was a lawyer on Wall Street and he and Grand-Dahlia and Mom lived in the City."

"Oh, my," Kath says sending a wink in my direction.

"I played...Central Park." Mom cocks her head, plants her hands on her hips, transforming herself into the fabled Eloise.

"Right." I offer more tea but Mom stops me, that devilish look in her eyes.

"Tell her who Daddy's good luck charm was."

Her pale eyelashes bat; she straightens her back and gives me the kind of smoldering look one would expect from Marilyn Monroe.

"Yes, Mom. You were his good luck charm. When he won in court he took you to Rumplemeyer's for jellybeans, then a ride in a hansom cab."

"Right!" she sits back, folds her hands in front of her like a little girl and asks for more tea and another scone. Thankfully, the story's finished.

Kathleen sits there smiling. "What a lovely story," she says, squeezing my shoulder as she prepares to leave.

"Please call so I can help out while your Mom's here." Then she kisses Mom, slips into her warm jacket and escapes.

Kathleen's kindness is endemic on this island. It's one of the reasons Mac and I have chosen to live out our lives here. "Simple people, simple pleasures," Mac had said when he asked me to make my life here with him. So what if I have to shovel snow off my roof once in awhile? At least I'm doing it with a man who still makes my socks roll up and down after twenty-eight years.

EIGHT

There is an incident with her shoes today that really breaks my heart. Mom has always made Imelda Marcos look like a novice. She hoards shoes, loves them, sometimes changing her shoes as often as six times in a day. She has shoes to match every outfit; my favorite being the red and white polka dot ones, which match her polka dot dress and hat. When I hear her screaming in her room, I race down to find her in tears, unable to tie her walking shoe, oblivious to the fact that she had a loafer on the other foot.

"Mom, your shoes don't match."

She looks down, realizes the mistake, and covers up by saying, "Yes, the brown one really needs polish." Then she sat on the edge of the bed and cried.

Later, Izzy calls. There's no mention of our previous conversation from Hell. That's the way it is with sisters, I guess.

"I was telling Mahatma how my conversation with you brought back a Tsunami wave of memories."

"Tsunami?" Christ, she always has to be so dramatic.

"You know, big wave, like they had in Indonesia."

"Jesus, Izzy, we get CNN in Canada." In the background, her wind chimes tinkle sweetly.

"Maybe it was the cup of tea that set me off. I started thinking about our little tea parties, the sugar cubes, those bone china teacups with the purple and yellow pansies. I get depressed just thinking about that."

"Me too, Iz, it's the pits."

Izzy doesn't participate in a two-way conversation. This is going to be one of her stream-of-consciousness calls so I listen carefully to her speech pattern to determine if I should pay attention, or continue with my chores while she talks. She's transitioning to her "mom" way of speaking; a little aloof, slightly aristocratic.

"I still have such visions of how Great-Grandpa traveled in a covered wagon until he arrived in a place to set up a town—a place they named Louisville."

"Uh-huh," I respond while walking around the room with a dust rag in one hand, a can of Pledge in the other.

"Remember how she lied and told us that the town was named after the Louisville Slugger baseball bat? And how Paul would sit there fidgeting in his coat and tie, then settle down and fall asleep right before the Derby came on the TV even though it was before supper?"

"Mmm, hmm." I'm sucking on my fifth tootsie pop of the day.

"What's killing me is the thought of our refined mother making a fool out of herself at the presentation in Louisville."

I check my reflection in the dining room table and watch as furrows track across my forehead. "You and me both."

"Mahatma's been urging me to talk about my feelings, admit my fear, that sort of thing." At this point I put the phone down, get a glass of water and return. She's still talking.

"Mahatma has a voice as soft as a cloud, Soph. She tells me to 'get it out' so gently that I almost think I'm back on the screen porch in Wisconsin and Mom is whispering for me to take a nap."

"Oh honey," I say. Here we go, I can feel it.

"Really Soph, I'm unable to shake away the images that I've kept buried for so long."

"Sweetie," I begin, worrying about her, as usual.

"Mahatma told me to have a cup of tea with my memories and I stayed in my lotus position for a long time. Then she brought me a steaming mug of Chamomile laced with organic honey." Iz's voice flows like syrup as she babbles.

"That's nice." The tinkling restarts.

"Then Mahatma plumped the silk pillows her mother had sent from Madras and directed me to relax."

Now I'm agitated. I really don't have time for her today.

"Know what, sis?" I really want to say 'earth to Izzy'.

"Hmmm?" she sort-of chants.

"Why don't you talk with Mahatma? I've got to do laundry and a million other things right now.

"Why aren't you ever there for me, Sophia?" Her whining cry flies from LA to PEI.

"Don't start that shit." I say. "Gotta go, Iz. Ciao for now." Click. Damn.

NINE

When I trot outside to fill my bird feeder, I'm pleasantly surprised by the temperature. It's unseasonably warm; there's no breeze off the ocean, which is quite cold this time of year. Where snow has melted, a fringe of new grass looks promising. I pause for a moment to inspect my south garden where most of the snow has melted. A parade of crocuses has appeared. I hope more will come while Mom is here.

Mac taps on the kitchen window holding up my favorite mug which is all the inspiration I need to return to the warmth of my house. The muffins I've baked with the last of my frozen blueberries are ready to come out of the oven. They smell so good that Mom is drawn from her bed. I'm relieved, because today we are having a yard sale and I really won't have much time for her.

After Mom gets dressed, she joins us in the yard. Our old clothing goes fast, scooped up by a woman with a large family who is pleased with the condition of our clothes and the low prices she's paid. As her husband carries the final load to their car, Mom blocks their way. "Put those back," she demands. "They belong to my daughter."

"No Mom, we don't need these any more. We've sold them to these people." I want to die.

Mom stands still as the concept crawls into her brain. Then, holding her head regally, she turns on me. "My dear, we *give* our clothes to the poor. We don't sell them." She snatches the ten dollar bill out of my hand and thrusts it into the husband's pocket. "There, there, she says," patting his back while escorting him to his car. "Have a nice day," she waves as I run into the house and burst into tears.

Later, after the last buyer has carted off our old bedroom set, we sit down to a pot of tea. I give Mom the day's take to count while Mac and I pack away the leftover items. She counts and counts, remarking how nice Queen Elizabeth looks on our Canadian dollars. Eventually, I ask how it's going and she puts her arms around the money on the table and with that toothy grin says, "It's mine, all mine." She continues to stack up the money in front of her and I realize that she's having trouble counting out the few hundred dollars. This makes me incredibly sad.

Without a doubt, Mom is gently slipping away and I see her behavior really begin to change. If she's upset by the fact that she's unable to count the money, she chooses to make better of the situation and turns it into a game. You have to smile and love her for it. I hope I don't sound too generous with my patience, because the truth is she drove me a little crazy today. Everywhere I went, she went and I mean *everywhere*. She followed me like a puppy, parroting my every move. If I straightened a chair, she did the same, again and again. For the hell of it I tilted my head to the left. She did the same. Mac came over to stop me, said I was being a jerk. I was, I am. But I want my mother back and she is lost in some terrible time warp—a state I know all too well.

TEN

I'm beginning to wonder if the trip is a good idea even though it's the result of months of planning. Mom has had this dream forever. For years, she's talked about getting all gussied up and presenting The Book. Just the thought of the fancy dinners and round of parties has had her chomping at the bit. Now I don't know what to do. She certainly can be dressed up, and her manners are so ingrained that she uses them by rote, but the thought of her making a fool of herself is more than I can bear.

Initially, Paul, Izzy and I planned to write out her remarks, adding our own personal greetings. However, I'm not sure how well she can read anymore. Or maybe she can read, but can't understand it. For example, we went out for lunch and she had to go to the bathroom. I followed to be on the safe side. Mom stood in front of the two doors, paused to read the sign that said "Men", then went in anyway. Of course I had to follow her in and turn her around, but not in time for a few heads to turn. And yes, their penises turned with them. Did she say anything? She sure did. My carefully-bred mother turned to her daughter with whom she never even discussed sex and said, "Seen one, you've seen them all".

I could ignore the whole thing; instead I try to explain to her why I'm so upset.

She shrugs it off. "Really dear, if you haven't seen a man drain his lizard by now, it's time you did."

Drain his lizard? I've never heard her say that before. And her speech patterns are so confusing. Sometimes she misses a word, uses the wrong word—and other times she can speak in sentences.

I call Paul; unload my concerns on him before he can say a word. Obviously, I'm interrupting his busy schedule so he dismisses this new evidence of her illness with that superior tone of his.

"She said drain his lizard…"

"Don't be vulgar, Sophia."

"Earth to Paw-Paw," I think I'll humor him.

"Like *you* have never gone into the wrong rest room?" he says impatiently. "Get a hold on yourself. You're probably just nervous about going on a long trip. This is not new for you— this is the Sophia I know. Remember how you used to pick fights with us before you tried something new? Remember?"

"I really hate you right now."

"Grow up! And stop making our mother out to be a drooling idiot. Izzy and I have sent you a crutch, which will make the trip a little easier. Hang in there."

He disconnects, just like he has his whole life.

Why is it that my brother has this amazing knack for turning everything upside down? Now it's time to psychoanalyze me. Talk about memory issues. He's forgotten that I didn't like to take car trips because I had a weak bladder and always had to stop to pee. Then there were the times when we were in traffic and couldn't stop and I'd wet myself. Paul and Izzy would punch me and say that I smelled, hold their noses, and scream out the window.

ELEVEN

Just when I'm starting to get down on myself, UPS pulls up at my door. Paul and Izzy have sent a cell phone, with a note that my brother will pay the bill. In another box there is a GPS system that I can plug in to my cigarette lighter. I've never used one before but Mac figures it out in a flash. I can't believe it, it actually talks! Fantastic! I feel much better knowing I can be in instant contact with someone while I make the long drive without Mac.

"Thank you so much, bro!" I hold the phone in my hand, marveling that it's mine.

"De Nada."

"Even though cell phone service may be spotty during the trip, who cares. I'm wired, baby. Cool, Paul. And the GPS is amazing. I'm pretty sure that I know my way to Belle Haven, but I've never been to Kentucky so this will be terrific!"

"Don't forget to thank Izzy too," he says, so I call her.

"Thanks so much for the stuff, Izzy. I'll feel much safer on the road now."

I hear ohm-ing in the background. Mahatma must be home.

"Well, Paul paid, but it was my idea. Let's face it, just because you live in Outer Mongolia doesn't mean you have to behave that way."

"Huh?" Is she coherent? Where is this coming from? Talk about passive aggressive.

"I was pissed at you for terrifying us about Mom, but then Mahatma reminded me that most perfectionists exaggerate to make a point." Her voice has developed a slight edge before she slams me.

"Listen, I can't really talk right now, I just wanted to thank you."

"Wait, Soph." She sounds panicky so I hang on. She clears her throat. "It's time for all of us to grow and this is a perfect moment. Admit it, you're a perfectionist who exaggerates, admit it."

I think for a moment. Hang up or be hanged. Shit.

"Whatever you say, Iz" I manage.

"Look, you're the same Sophia who told Papa I was a veritable drug addict when I was just smoking a few joints on weekends."

Nice, I call to thank her and we are going to rehash old crap. I decide to indulge her with a reasonable explanation.

"It was quite a bit worse than that, Iz. You were a fifteen-year old kid who was sliding down a very slippery slope.

"You and Jack were doing some pretty heavy drinking, that's for sure."

"We were college kids, for God's sake."

"Yes, but you told Mom and Papa and they made my life hell."

"So I apologize," I say dying to get off the phone.

"Good. Now, admit that you're exaggerating about Mom," says my sister trying to sound like a shrink but instead sounding like a whining brat.

"Yeah, right—whatever you need to believe. Just remember, I'm the one who's here with her."

Click. That's what I get for trying to be gracious.

***

Just when I wish I didn't have a sister, I notice her photograph on the mantel over our fireplace. This one was taken about a year ago when she and Mahatma first met. She's a beautiful woman, for sure, clearly the looker in our family. She looks a lot like my father. Her eyes are the same dark blue as his with pale green and yellow around the irises. She has his strong jaw and deep dimples, just a gorgeous woman. In this photograph she's let her hair grow to below her shoulders. I look closer. Her skin is pretty wrinkled now, between the sun and the drugs and maybe genetics. Mom's side is all pruney. Still, with her California tan, she looks sensational. She's wearing a dashiki that hides her figure. She's built like Mom, small-breasts and slim hips; a girl's body really. Mac's glad that I take after the Italian side, more curvy and buxom.

I reach for the phone.

"Izzy, I'm looking at your photograph."

"Which one?" A gong chimes in the background.

"The one you sent me from Big Sur. You look beautiful."

"Well photos lie. Everyone out here gets peeled and pulled and tucked and I don't rule it out, just not right now while I'm living paycheck to paycheck."

"I don't believe what I'm hearing," I say. This is natural girl I'm talking to.

"Well, it's a sign of my evolving that I would even consider cosmetic surgery. I mean, I'm the girl who burned her bra and chanted "God is coming and SHE is pissed!"

I have to laugh. I love my sister, no matter if she embraces every cause and hangs onto it far too long. She's a good sport though.

"Do you still have the T-shirt?"

"Of course I do." She gave me my all time favorite T-shirt

of hers that she got at a feminist rally in Berkeley. It's faded now but you can still make out its prophetic message: "A woman without a man is like a fish without a bicycle". Gloria Steinem was her idol. I wonder if Gloria still believes this now that she's married to someone who's supposed to be a terrific guy.

When I think about Gloria Steinem it brings me back to Mom. She was part of the Revolution too. She always was very vocal about Women's Rights, wrote dozens of letters to Congress supporting equal opportunities for women and was also a big believer in Civil Rights. Mom marched in support of everything that brought about fairness. It's ironic that God has dealt her an unfair hand.

TWELVE

Mac, Mom and I go to a ceilidh at the church meeting hall where she can hear the fiddlers and watch the Islanders dance. This informal get-together is one of her favorite activities when she comes to visit. For years, we've tried to get her onto the dance floor but she's been contented to sit and sip her toddy, listen to the fiddlers and watch the merriment.

Tonight we have a surprise. We're not there more than fifteen minutes when she grabs Mac, pulls him off his seat and demands that he dance with her. As God as my witness my mother did the meanest step dance I'd ever seen. Even the Islanders circled around to watch her kick up her heels and stomp.

"You've been practicing, Agatha Rose," Mac shouts over the fiddles.

She whispers something in his ear. Mac turns red as an apple, a look of shock and amusement covering his face.

"What did she whisper to you?" I ask when they return to their seats.

"You don't want to know," my husband says.

"What?"

"I couldn't even hear her," he lied.

"Hmmm," I said knowing that he'll never tell. That's how Mac is.

Later, Mom and I wrap thick shawls knitted by Kathleen's mother around our shoulders, then step outside to look at the new moon.

"Do you remember what Neil Armstrong said when he set foot on the moon?" I'm just making conversation, not expecting a rational answer.

"Of course I do, dear," she answers so sweetly that I'm embarrassed I asked.

"Free at last, free at last, thank George almighty I'm free at last!" Well, she's close.

"No Mom that was Martin Luther King. Neil Armstrong said 'one small step for man; one giant step for mankind'". Mom's face wears a wonderful expression.

"And he was right, wasn't he?" she says. I don't push. I'm not sure whom she is referring to but it doesn't matter. Certainly, both of these men were right.

I remember how she wept when Martin Luther King was assassinated. Mom adored that man. She'd heard him speak in person one time when she was visiting a professor friend at Boston University and never forgot it. "He just might be the most important man of this century," she had remarked just days before his death. For years, Mom listened to his "I Have a Dream" speech until we all knew it by heart. She was utterly brilliant, with almost a photographic memory so I can't imagine what it will do to her if she really has Alzheimer's. It's unacceptable. Absolutely not fair.

THIRTEEN

I t's around noon and I'm having a ball. I've been up all night decorating the Shaughnessy's wedding cake. It's several shades of yellow and I've hand-painted portraits of their dogs (honest) at their request.

Jack's mother had taught me how to bake and even gave me some of her secret recipes. We worked for hours in her little kitchen, turning out petit fours, rum babas and delicate cookies. She had offered to teach and I had wanted to learn. Anything to stay close to Jack.

Her lessons were long ago and much of what she taught me I still follow to the "T". Her bread-baking technique was inimitable; try as I might, I have never mastered it. Fondly, I think of her making a simple, crusty French loaf to accompany the beef stew she served the last time I saw her. I can still hear the sound of her kneading and pounding, slapping the dough onto a floured marble slab until she was satisfied. Finally she had held up the dough for me to touch. "The staff of life," she had whispered before she plopped it into a greased bowl and covered it with cheesecloth. I had insisted on cleaning up, giving her time to catch her breath and wipe the tears from her eyes. Then, leaving everything unspoken, we sipped from water glasses filled with wine, staying close by each other as the warmth from her double oven penetrated the chill in the room. The next morning, as Mac and I prepared to leave, she had pressed one more recipe into my hand—the treasured family secret passed down from her grandmother.

Today, my lemon pound cake is the most sought-after wedding cake on the Island. It's loaded with butter and sugar, guaranteed to find a home on your hips, but simply delicious. I call it Patrice's Heritage Cake, and I think of her whenever I bake.

FOURTEEN

Mom is fascinated by my work, and makes me feel good as she compliments my creation! Momentarily, that is. The good feelings evaporate when she points to a dog and asks "What's that?"

Mom loves dogs, especially Rodney, our old basset hound. She would sit on the floor with that smelly old dog for hours, tying and untying his ears, singing, *"Do your ears hang low, do they wobble to and fro? Can you tie them in a knot; can you tie them in a bow? Can you throw them over your shoulder like a continental soldier; do your ears hang low?"*...One of the dogs I've hand-painted is a basset hound. Mom thinks it's a horse. I'm not going to bother to tell the Great Pretenders these details anymore. They can live in denial if they want to, but I'm here to see it. So is Mac.

Speaking of dogs, I take an extra minute to bring a soup bone outside for the neighbor's dog who likes to sunbathe on my front steps. It's a beautiful day; cloudless sky, unseasonably warm, a great day for a wedding. I hum Aretha's "Chain of Fools" as I pull the car up to the front door, still humming until I walk through my front door and see what she's done.

In the three minutes that she was out of my sight, Mom has sliced a piece of the wedding cake and is taking her last bite!

I grab her hand and shake it hard. "Oh my God, are you trying to wreck my business? What in hell are you thinking?" I scream as my blood pressure goes through the roof.

Mom smiles at me and then laughs. "I'm glad I did it, you stupid cow, it's delicious!" Then her face goes blank and she stares off into space. I am shocked at the level of my rage, afraid that I am going to swat her. I have to pinch myself hard to remember that this woman is totally clueless. But there is this ugly part of me that hates her for being sick, for being here, for being my mother. Talk about Chain of Fools.

I call Izzy.

"What can I say to make you feel better, Sophia?" she asks in her shrink voice.

"Nothing."

"Can you fix the cake?" She knows I can, I'm sure of it.

"Okay, okay. So I know how to fix the damn cake. That's not the point, Izzy."

"I know. So tell me how you'll fix it."

"I sent Mac to the store to buy a yellow cake. Then I'll cut a slice the same size, whip up some more frosting and fake it."

"You're a genius," she breathes.

"Yeah, more like mad genius," I say. And then I remember that Halloween and it all comes creeping back.

FIFTEEN

J ack, Mac and I had decided to go trick-or-treating in one of the more fancy neighborhoods of Ann Arbor. Jack and Mac's costumes were pre-determined, so they focused on me. At first, Colonel Parker said, "She should go as Priscilla." It sounded good to me, but Jack had something different up his sleeve. "No, she'll go as a mad genius and we get to dress her up." I didn't find the idea appealing, but I was curious to see what they would come up with.

Minutes later, after raiding a janitor's closet, they appeared. Jack was carrying a pillowcase stuffed with my costume. They had stolen a stringy mop head for my hair. Then they pasted black hockey stick tape on my eyebrows. Mac produced an old pair of glasses that were bottle thick and Jack made me put on his pajama bottoms, black suit coat, sweaty T-shirt and a necktie. I felt like a complete idiot, but they loved it. When I kept tripping over Jack's pajama bottoms, he picked me up and carried me door-to-door. That was the first time I noticed how good he smelled, a combination of Old Spice and Jack.

When we returned to campus, someone took our picture. It appeared in the campus newspaper that weekend. The caption under the photo read, "Our Elvis and the Colonel return to campus with Halloween treats." There was no mention of me. Not then.

I'm beginning to see a pattern with these flashbacks. It seems that they arrive every time I am under real stress.

SIXTEEN

Today has been a day for discovery. Before going to bed, I decide to inspect Mom's purse. In it I find bits of leftover dinners wrapped very carefully in napkins, Kleenex, whatever. I hate to think how long they've been there.

"Are you saving this Mom?" I ask, showing her a dried-up piece of meat.

She pauses. "No, it's for the——. " She reaches for words that don't come.

Bringing twenty-three pairs of underwear is not as absurd as I first thought. Little did I know that she would be hiding them instead of putting them in the wash. I find them in the trash can, bureau drawers, her suitcase, corners of her room and bathroom, her purse, between the mattress and box spring, and places I'm sure I haven't discovered. Some of her panties show that she's had minor mishaps and maybe she's embarrassed, but most haven't, so I think she just likes to hide them.

***

Early the next morning, Mac and I head to the beach for a little quiet time before Mom arises. The landscape is tinted in washed-out shades of blue-gray except for the fog over the water, which is smoky, almost white. A flock of laughing gulls swoop over the surface until they spot a school of fish. They cry to each other while diving to skim the surface, and then follow the fish all the way down the beach. We sip coffee from thermoses and nibble our scones. Mac's on his third one before I remind him that they're loaded with butter. He doesn't pay attention, just woofs it down, taking a swig of coffee before letting out an appreciative belch.

I look toward the sea, imprinting the beauty of my surroundings, just as I do before every trip that takes me away from my Island. It's times like this when I put everything in perspective. If we're tight for cash like most Islanders are at some time or another, I look at the sea, or to my gardens and imagine what it would be like if I had no sight. That thought banishes any worries. I'm truly grateful and feel very blessed to live my life here with this wonderful man who stands beside me.

When we return home, Mac announces that he's taking "his girls" out for lunch.

"Want to go to Captain Neptune's, Agatha Rose?" He flashes those dimples, puts his arm around her waist and she claps her hands.

"Oh goodie," she says slipping into her coat. When she sees me put on my jacket she turns to Mac. "Does *she* have to come?"

Mac sees that I'm crestfallen, never mind that my mother is ill. So he whispers in her ear, "She'd have my ass if I ever went out alone with such a good lookin' babe."

"Yeah, Mom," I chime in trying to set aside my hurt feelings, "people would talk if my husband's seen around town with a hot chick."

We park in front of the restaurant and Mom's very excited. She remembers the place from her last trip. As we enter, the smell of beer and onions hits us in the face; the crowd is rowdy and the smoke is thick. Still, we put up with it since they serve the best lobster rolls in Charlottetown.

Eating out or just sitting in a public place is becoming tricky business. Mom likes to keep a running commentary on other diners. As we dive into our burgers, Mom notices a waitress carrying a dessert piled high with whipped cream. Mom's eyes follow the dessert to the table where a large woman is sitting with her family. As the woman takes her first mouthful, Mom says in a voice loud enough to be heard by everyone, "Now she *would* order that! No wonder she's so fat!" There was no way the woman didn't hear her and there was no place to hide. This is becoming a serious issue. Mom was never catty or rude in her life. Her behavior is so out-of-character that it's hard to believe. I'll have to find a way to control her from sharing all her observations out loud.

When I report this to Izzy she cackles, "Leave it to old Mom to tell it like it is! Hilarious!"

"It's a real riot," I say, "especially when she slapped my face after I told her to mind her manners."

"Oh," Izzy says.

"And there's more. A little girl walked by our table and quick as a wink Mom reached up and pulled her pigtail, and then looked away when the girl screamed."

"Whew, Soph, sounds like you've got your hands full."

"Never mind me. How could our gentle mother become mean and cruel? What kind of a God does this to a person who has only done good things in her life?" Izzy has no answer. She's heard me question God many times. Mac, too.

SEVENTEEN

W here in God's name are we?" Mac had asked repeatedly from the moment we had turned onto the dirt road that ran for a quarter of mile toward the lake. Jack had brought a good flashlight; still, we were deep in the Wisconsin woods, looking for the path that lead to the old summer cottage that Grand Dahlia had left to Mom. I had promised them a week of fun in the sun where we could swim and canoe and celebrate the end of our junior year before going off to our summer jobs. We hadn't planned to see each other until the following September.

Mac and Jack agreed that the cottage was everything I'd described, and more. The place was rustic and without frills, a place to put your feet up, crack open a cold beer and a good book and let the world pass you by. During the day, we hiked through the pine forests, paddled the old canoe along the shore and swam in the icy lake. At night, we cooked huge feasts, followed by campfires on the beach, where we sang the latest songs and stuffed ourselves with s'mores.

Since there was no television, we entertained ourselves by telling ghost stories. Hands down, Jack's were the scariest. With his clever, creative mind, Jack could terrify us in minutes. He would point out shadows on the wall, drop a book behind the sofa, and make odd whistling sounds that drove Mac and me to scramble under quilts, hiding our feet and hands, and curling into fetal positions. Some nights I'd be so scared that I'd beg

Jack not to tell a story. It wasn't until later that I realized he'd enjoyed scaring me on the chance that I'd rush into his arms for comfort. Sometimes, he'd even plant a soft kiss on top of my head.

Jack couldn't pronounce "th". He'd say "dem" for "them", "doze" for "those" and so on. So when he turned to me after Jack had taken the boat out to the middle of the lake and said, "Deez are da best days off my life," I started to giggle nervously. Somehow I knew what Jack meant. Yet I also knew that we three were the best of friends and that coupling off could ruin it. Still, when Jack reached to pull me into his arms, I knew I wanted to be there. Jack later claimed that he checked his watch and waited a full five minutes before I tilted my head and waited for his kiss. We were barely able to stop ourselves until a car door slammed and Paul appeared, a guitar case in one hand, a bag of groceries in the other.

"Mom said I could come for the weekend," he said sheepishly.

"Ah," Jack grunted, and for the first time since he'd met my little brother, he didn't seem overjoyed to greet him. Our cool reception zoomed right past Paul, who was proud that he was allowed to take his first long trip with Mom's car after passing his driving test. So our quiet, tuning-out vacation turned raucous and boyish with me being the target of practical jokes and relentless teasing. Jack seemed embarrassed by his show of affection towards me and I turned moody. To retaliate, I whipped up a version of Mom's Derby Pie and tripled the amount of bourbon called for in the recipe. Finally, I had a peaceful evening, as the three of them snored on the couches.

EIGHTEEN

Y ou're snoring," Mac says as he tucks the afghan under my chin. I'd fallen asleep on the sofa, warmed by the penetrating heat of our woodstove.

"I don't snore," I lie, embarrassed for some vain reason. As I awaken, I smell something great coming from the kitchen. Mac has made a fresh pot of coffee. After watching me sniff and smile, he brings me a cup.

"Getting excited about the trip?" he asks, settling in beside me.

"A little apprehensive, I'm afraid."

"Babe, it will be wonderful if you can fulfill her dream. All you have to do is get her down there in one piece, dress her up, fork over the book then go to the Kentucky Derby. Piece of cake."

He's right, and I relax with my coffee until my skin starts to prickle. "I just had a thought. What if I can't find the book when we get to Mom's? Maybe she left it at the airport or has hidden it somewhere. This could be a disaster—".

"Or the most important trip of your life," he says so softly I strain to hear him.

"I'm scared shitless."

"You'll be fine, hon." He tweaks the tip of my nose before planting a loud, smacking kiss on both cheeks.

Uh huh.

Later, we take Mom to the curling club so she can watch curling. She loves this sport, thinks it's the stupidest, funniest thing in the world. She has never understood the game. Now it's worse.

"Why is someone taking a broom to the ice?" Why are they doing that?" she asks over and over.

"It's how the game is played, Mom." But that's not the end of it.

"Do fishermen play?"

"Yes Mom, I suppose they do." What on earth is she thinking?

"Then you lied?" Her eyes glint and she's angry with me for what I don't know.

"What do you mean, Mom, lied about what?"

"You said where you live there are only two things you can do in the winter. Fish or diddle. And in the winter you don't fish."

She has managed to get out those sentences, clearly, without garbling one single word. Still, I'm shocked. I would never say such a thing to my mother.

"Mom!" I don't know if I'm angry with her or furious because the lack of inhibition is one of the key behaviors in Alzheimer's.

"Sophia's been lying every once in awhile, Aggie Ro," Mac says sweetly. "We let her get away with it because she's getting older, you know."

Mom scrunches up her nose, draws down her eyebrows and tries to hide the tears in her eyes. "I can't believe you are calling my...*her*...a liar," she sobs. Then she stops, and stares at Mac. "Who are *you*?" Mac is about to answer when she turns her attention back to the game, pointing and laughing, elbowing Mac and me. Oh, God.

Paul calls and I relish the opportunity to blow off steam.

"You're really wonderful to take Mom to Louisville," he schmoozes.

Then he lies and says he'd go with us if he could. To frost the cake, he says Izzy would too. Now that would be a trip. I can see the headlines now...*Siblings die, leaving confused mother alone in car.*..The autopsy would show that we all died hoarse with pierced eardrums.

Then he surprises me. "You know that I'm scared that she's dying and there's so much more living for her to do."

"I know bro."

"You won't believe this but I'm actually going to take a vacation! I'm planning on taking Mom to the theatre in New York next Christmas, Radio City, Rockefeller Center, the whole deal. Just get her to Louisville and back home in one piece. Then we'll deal with this, Soph, promise."

There's something else I hear in his voice, something he's not saying.

NINETEEN

I don't know what ever possessed me to think that I could do this, especially without Mac. I suppose it's because of ignorance of the disease and denial, denial, denial.

For the first hour on the road all she talks about is my niece, Fiona, whom she swears she speaks to every night. It's very tender hearing how a grandmother loves a grandchild, unequivocally. There is no mention of the drugs, the overdoses, and the pain. Nothing.

As a treat, I choose to take the new Confederation Bridge—a marvel of engineering which links our island to the mainland. This means a nine-mile drive across the Northumberland Strait where Mom can see chunks of ice that have floated down from the north. Since she doesn't pay much attention to the bridge, it's more of a treat for me than for her. The bridge is pretty amazing when you think of it. Imagine taking ten minutes to drive across a bridge at fifty miles an hour with no traffic! The center span climbs fairly high and the view is breathtaking. It would have been nice to have a spot to pull over, turn around and look back at the red cliffs of Prince Edward Island.

"Isn't this amazing, Mom?"

She nods, nothing more. Well, trust me. It *is* amazing. The bridge curves gently until we reach New Brunswick where we proceed west on the TransCanada Highway. She's amused that all of the highway signs are in French and English, but the billboard signs are mostly in French. "Que sera sera," she says each time she sees a billboard. And there are lots of billboards.

I point out skimobile trails until I realize that she doesn't know what a skimobile is. So I choose to be silent, to let her be alone with her thoughts, knowing that her surroundings can offer her peace. The landscape is beautiful, even more so as we head southwest. There are open fields fringed with spruce forests, then long rolling hills that stretch on for miles. The sun's reflection on the snow-covered wonderland is dazzling. Yet now, I think of the blazing white light that people report when they've had a near-death experience. I shudder as I reach for a bottle of water, suddenly parched.

TWENTY

The full impact of this trip has really hit home. Driving intensifies a closeness that was softened by diversions and space when we were on the Island. At times, I look over and really focus on my mother. Her posture, which once emanated grace and elegance, now is slightly bent. Despite being 5'10", she appears frail and small, and dammit, she looks vulnerable. I'm overwhelmed by how lost she appears. She stares out the window for hours with a vacant look in her eyes. I wonder where she has gone, what she's thinking about.

It's going to be a long, long drive. I call the kids on the cell phone—and ask them to pray for us.

Conversation is futile so I try to get her to sing along with me. *"Over the river and through the woods, to grandmother's house we go"*...Nothing. We pass a flock of chickens and she clucks.

"I love the way you made our Thanksgiving turkey, Mom. No one makes turkey better than when you lay bacon strips over the skin."

She sticks out her tongue. "Eck". It's like talking to a stranger.

"So, what would you like to eat for dinner tonight?"

"D.V.O.T."

D.V.O.T. means "dog vomit on toast" a phrase from her boarding school days. So her long-term memory is working some of the time.

We stop at the Moose n' Goose Grill. Mom takes special notice of the mounted moose heads lining the walls.

"What sound does a moose make?" she asks.

I look around the empty restaurant to be sure I'm out of earshot, then snort three times and whistle.

"Really, how frightening," Mom says, satisfied with the answer. "Is there anything you don't know, Sonia?" Mom reaches across the table to squeeze my hand and I burst out crying. She's forgotten my name.

TWENTY-ONE

After a good night's sleep we cross into Quebec, passing through the small town of St.-Louis-du-Ha-Ha. The name of the town cracks Mom up. She extends her hand and says, "Hello, I'm from St. Louis du Ha Ha. A beat. Ha, ha!" And again. And again, until she announces, "I made tinkle in my bloomers."

Shit. There are no gas stations, restaurants, and rest areas. We're out in the effing country! I pull over, get her out of the car and learn that she loves pulling off her panties in broad daylight! I toss them ceremoniously toward a bird that flies by. Back on the road, she laughs some more until we reach Riviere-du-Loup on the edge of the St. Lawrence Seaway.

"We're headed toward Quebec City, Mom. Maybe we can go into the old city and find a wonderful French restaurant."

"I don't want to," she says. This is the woman who taught our Basque cook to make a coq au vin to rival Julia Child's. I choke up; then again she's probably right but for the wrong reasons. We need to make time. Instead, we pull in to a roadside diner where I order for us poutine, a Quebequois specialty of French fries smothered in melted cheese and topped with gravy. I ignore the obvious danger of this artery-clogging, cholesterol-laden dish, to say nothing of the calories, and clean my plate.

When we get back on the road Mom is quiet, ignoring my attempts at conversation. At this point, I settle for the silence to focus on the road ahead. Suddenly, she shrieks, "Stop!"

I try to assess the problem while pulling over to stop the car.

There's no traffic anywhere, nothing in the road, Mom isn't bleeding or vomiting or otherwise oozing. Still, she's yelling, "Stop, stop, stop."

She's having a heart attack, I just know it. "Mom, What is it?" I release my seatbelt while searching for anything and everything that might be wrong, "Are you hurt?"

She points out the window to a snowfield where a few cows are grazing on clumps of hay, sighs dramatically and says, "There!"

"*What?*" I ask, scanning.

Mom's expression tells me that she thinks I'm on another planet. "The eeny weeny baby cow," I have a sudden urge to use every four-letter word I know. Instead, I scold her.

"Mom, you screamed at me. I could have had an accident."

"But it's so cute!" she says with the wonderment of a child.

I can't say anything, I'm afraid there might be bloodshed yet. I take a few deep breaths, clear my throat and swallow hard. When the calf works its way over to the fence to check us out, I can't help but chuckle. Then I laugh a little louder until Mom joins in, pointing at the curious calf. Mom laughs and points, while slugging my arm to be sure I see what she sees. Our adrenaline rises as we laugh harder, hers from excitement and mine, well, let's just say from a wide range of emotions!

The rest of the afternoon she's content just to count cows as we drive through farmland. "Oh my, there are, let's see, one, two, three, four, five brown and white cows." That's when she can keep the math straight. She often skips seven, goes from six to eight.

When she isn't on cow alert, she becomes rather fixated on Canadian money, and when we can get rid of it! "We're in Quebec now, get out the real money!"

I explain ad nauseum that Quebec is still in Canada despite their attempts to secede and therefore we still need to use Canadian dollars, which by the way, is real money. Then we get the map out and I show her where we left from, where we're going and the route we're taking to her house.

"Oh, the lake house...? How nice!"

Perhaps I sound like a bitch. I certainly feel like one, but here's a snippet of our conversation today—the one repeated at least nine times before I stopped counting.

"Aren't we going to the Derby?"

"Yes, but we have to go home and get your book."

"What book?"

"The family book."

"I brought it."

"You brought a book on the Alhambra! We need to get the family history book to give to the Historical Society, so we are going to Wisconsin first."

"Have we left the Island?"

"Yes."

"Goodie, we can use real money."

We stop at Le Chateau diner where we order meatloaf and mashed potatoes. When dinner comes she takes out her partial dentures and plops them in a glass of water. As people walk by she holds up her glass and shouts, "Have a dink." As we were leaving she lifted her sweater and flashed an old man who was entering the diner. All I can do is laugh and shudder at the thought of what's to come.

When we return to our room, I make a beeline to the shower, leaving the bathroom door open in case she decides to walk outside, or worse. As I stand there soaping up, I realize that Mom is talking to the television set. An old Lassie movie is on tonight.

"Here boy, here boy. Eat your foo-fee." This is the woman I'm taking to an elegant function in Louisville. I only know that I'd rather die than have her humiliate herself.

Mac calls before I close my eyes. I don't know what I would do without his gentle words, encouragement and patient ears. Before collapsing, I power up my laptop, so I can check on orders and ask Kath to help out if she can. Mom loves the sound of America Online hooking up. I tell her it's the sound of the mailman of the millennium. She tells me she once had an affair with a mailman. We'll never know.

TWENTY-TWO

Today we're continuing on our southwest route driving beside the Ottawa River. Luckily, we're heading to flat farmland where we're bound to find enough cows to keep her entertained. At this point I've had to remove the GPS because whenever it "speaks" Mom goes crazy, searching through the glove compartment for the little woman who's stuck inside.

Just as she's about to get bored, I spot some dots on the horizon. Bingo! A herd of black and white cows appears on her side of the car. There are mommy cows and baby cows; we are in luck! Mom sticks her head out the window, moos at them, moos at me, and sticks out her tongue, and then laughs for a good five minutes before she dozes off.

When I'm able to analyze my feelings I realize that I'm scared and mad about the hand Fate has dealt her. I love Mom and I'm losing her. I just pray that this trip isn't speeding up the process because she seems to be much worse than she was on the Island.

I email the kids, why, I'm not sure. Maybe I'm looking to make a point, or maybe I just want some sympathy. Or maybe I want them to acknowledge that I'm being a martyr—again.

TWENTY-THREE

This is one time you don't have to suck it up and put on your martyr suit," Izzy had said when I announced my plans to return to college a week after the accident. "Come to Haight with me before I start at Berkeley," I remember her saying, as if it were yesterday.

A month after he'd left our Wisconsin cottage, Jack hitchhiked back to so he could court me in style. Style to Jack meant weaving garlands of wildflowers for me to wear on my head and around my neck. It meant long canoe rides with a transistor radio playing our favorite songs. It meant making love under a canopy of stars, then falling asleep on the beach. Jack and I fell in love so hard and so fast we were giddy and breathless, unable to keep our hands off each other while marveling at the depth of our feelings.

After only a week of being together as a couple, Jack proposed to me in Grand Dahlia's canoe. I was totally unsuspecting when we paddled to the middle of the lake to watch the sunset. He'd brought along ham and cheese sandwiches, cokes, and a big bag of Wise potato chips. For dessert, we munched on chocolate chip cookies that Mom had given him after he had clued her in about the big moment.

The ring had been his grandmother's; a perfect Burmese ruby surrounded by tiny diamonds set in an intricate rose gold setting. Jack's hand had trembled when he slid the heirloom onto my finger. "For my future wife," he'd announced proudly, as he stared at the ring on my left hand. He was shaking his head in disbelief, amazed that I'd said 'yes'.

We spent the next day on the telephone calling Mac who was back in Bangor with his phantom girlfriend, talking to friends and family and planning a date. We settled easily on a casual wedding the following summer in Mom's garden, with a reception that would be more of a hoe down than a formal affair. In fact, breaking from tradition, Jack deemed it okay to have best "men". Mac and Paul would share a place of honor. Jack's mother would bake the cake.

Paul and Izzy were thrilled. For Paul, it meant having a big brother whom he already adored. Izzy had developed a mad crush on Jack, so she pretended to sulk until I asked her to be my maid of honor. My father, bless him, offered enough summer employment to Jack so he could stay with me in Wisconsin. It was a magical time for all of us.

Our plans for the fall had already been set before Jack and I fell in love. Jack, Mac and I had signed a lease on a great apartment in an old Victorian near the campus. Several other friends had apartments nearby. We were so excited by the prospect of being together that we planned to move in a week early, right after returning from our trip to Jack's home near Squam Lake in New Hampshire.

I feel dizzy remembering those days and now it's hard for me to breathe. Road trips have a way of bringing it all back, as if it were yesterday. That must be what's going on here.

TWENTY-FOUR

Mom and I are off after a long breakfast at a greasy diner where she takes almost an hour to eat one egg, one English muffin and drink one cup of coffee. I have to remind her to take her diabetes medication and vitamins. Finally, we get in the car and she calls me Izzy. With all due respect to Izzy, I have tits, she doesn't.

The drive begins with what is becoming our routine. Mom can be quite chatty now especially if we talk about her earlier years. Even though her word retrieval is deteriorating more each day, she bumps past it. Mom shares many wonderful memories and though maybe some are a little embellished, none more than any good story would be expanded upon over many years. Almost always, the hero of the story is Gramps.

Actually, I must admit I try to take a little advantage of this situation. There has always been a dark mystery surrounding Grandpa and Mom's relationship. There have been ample innuendoes and fleeting references to it, but "the grownups" always kept their secrets well guarded.

So, here we are driving down the highway, with Mom reminiscing about the good old days, all with fairly good accuracy, so I decide to seize the moment. "Tell me about your debut," I suggest hopefully.

"No."

"Why not?"

"No." The wall goes up fast. I don't doubt for a moment that she knows exactly what I mean. It's simply her instincts at work. She and the elders of the family swore to take this secret to their graves and no amount of coaxing, bribing or dementia will produce loose lips. Some things are just too ingrained.

Southbury is up ahead and it's nearing 4:00.

"You drive good, Isabela" Mom says.

I say, "No Mom, I'm not Izzy; I'm Sophia, your oldest".

She's adamant." Don't be silly Darlin, Sophia lives in Canada." So I just settle in, play the game. I guess she misses Iz.

Although the cows are no longer evident, there are enough horses and goats to keep her occupied. I no longer slam on the brakes when she commands me to pull over. I just drive along, play along. It's not so bad unless she throws a tantrum.

I'm so relaxed that I almost doze off at the wheel.

"I need a nap, Mom" I explain as I pull off the road.

"Promise that you'll stay right next to me."

"Course I will." As I'm about to doze off I feel her warm breath near my mouth. She kisses me softly, strokes my cheek then begins to curl my hair. Tears cloud my eyes. She's my mommy again.

Then, in that sweet wonderful voice of hers she sings, *"A dream is a wish your heart makes, when you're fast asleep."* She hums the rest but I don't care. I'm in heaven, so peaceful and relaxed that I barely hear her say, "Take nappy nap, Mommy."

After a fifteen-minute nap I'm able to drive for another three hours before calling it quits. I start watching for a motel when my cell phone rings. Izzy sounds upset.

She says "You really need to kewl it". Not cool it, the way we all spoke growing up, but now with an LA, (she says el-LAY) accent. Here she goes, the blind leading the blind.

"I spoke to Paul today and he was so zonked he could barely speak. He's been working eighteen hour days for weeks, so it doesn't look like he'll be able to even think about meeting up with you in Wisconsin. He feels guilty, said you called and laid a huge guilt trip on him."

"Since when are you his keeper?"

She says, "We'll solve our immediate problems on the phone."

Immediate problems—that's a bit formal for Izzy-speak. Probably she took notes from Paul.

"Paul's going to try to get to Wisconsin this summer; when he can maybe do some work around the house. Until then, let's all try being kinder and gentler with each other." Honest, that's what Izzy said.

Now you have to know Izzy. Speaking with her is like having a conversation with several people, not just my baby sister. She suffers from some sort of fragmented thinking in that she takes on many different personalities in a conversation. During one of our conversations last summer I thought I was talking with Mao Tse Tung; another time, it was Queen Elizabeth. When she was in her death and dying phase she was Elisabeth Kubler-Ross; her healthy phase it was Andrew Weil; her fat phase she was Dr. Atkins, the author of the South Beach Diet and Florine Marks, the Weight Watchers queen, rolled into one.

Ah, but that's the *sane* Izzy. Then we have what Grand Dahlia would call her "spells". In these spells, brought on by substance abuse in any form she can get her hands on, we might hear Ferlinghetti poetry, quotes from Rolling Stones lyrics, she'll sing, sounding like a cross between Janis Joplin and Stevie Nicks.

I call her back because I need to have the last word. I've thought of a zinger. I say, "Before I forget, Izzy, have you been to any meetings lately? What's the meeting-of-the-week this week? Sex and love addicts anonymous?"

"Go to Hell." Izzy draws out each word slowly, like a fingernail across a blackboard.

And in el-lay speak, I add, "Who are you hangin' with these days?"

When I hang up I don't feel any better.

TWENTY-FIVE

I've been to Southbury before and remember it as a rough and dirty mining town. I really want to get through it before dark. On the outskirts of town, the land is dry, dusty and desolate. We pass a rundown motel complete with screen door swinging in the wind on one hinge and balls of twigs and old plastic shopping bags blowing in the dust. "Norman, Norrrrman"—I think of Tony Perkins' psycho mother calling. Just beyond, I see a gas station and decide I'll fill up before I get into rush hour traffic. I think it might start earlier with mine shifts.

So I pull in, fill up, pay and try to shift into first. No go. I keep trying, any gear will do. No luck. Mom says, "Let's go dear."

"Give me a second." My heart starts to flutter. I try again. Nothing.

I get the attendant. He comes out and jumps in the car, ready to try and shift. Mom shrieks, "Get out of my car! Who the hell do you think you are?"

The attendant levitates out of his seat, scared to death. I try to calm Mom. "This nice man is trying to help us."

She's not buying it. In the meantime, the attendant pops the hood to peer into the engine. Mom is quiet with the distraction of the hood up and her view blocked. Phew.

He mutters something about the transmission then pounds on something in the engine.

Mom screams, "Stop hitting my car, you bastard! Get away!" And on and on. "Screw you, pisshole! Scram, shitbum!"

Who is this woman who has replaced my mother?

I am speechless and he's just looking at me, maybe wondering if I was going to start attacking him, too. Finally, I blurt out "Alzheimer's. I'm so sorry. I'll calm her down."

He nods, "Same with my little woman."

While I talk to her through the window, he closes the hood and jumps in the car. "I'm taking it down the road to see if I can get the gears moving."

Amazingly, he is able to slam it into gear and drive off. He is now unfazed that Mom is in the car with him, still hollering at the top of her lungs.

All of a sudden, there I am, standing alone at the gas pump in the blowing dust listening to Mom's yells fading down the road. What has just happened here? Mom must be terrified. He must be terrified. Maybe he has kidnapped her or is trying to steal the car. If that's the case, he's crazy and I wish him luck because I have the feeling Mom will get the best of him.

They weren't long; I can hear Mom still yelling at him as they come up the road. He jumps out. "The transmission has seized."

Wonderful.

Tom, as I come to know him, couldn't be nicer or more helpful. Well, it certainly isn't difficult to see the extent of my troubles. He has a friend who owns a motel down the road, (not the *Psycho* one we passed). "I'll call around in the morning to see if I can find a garage to fix the car, then I'll tow it over."

This motel may only be slightly better than the Bates Motel, but it has two beds and a phone in the room. There's a food counter near the front desk so at least we can get something to eat. Mind you, Mom is happy to sip on bourbon for a while! Later, we sit outside in rickety chairs watching the traffic go by. We're too tired to speak, however, as evening falls and the motel fills up, I realize that this is a motel mainly for transient miners! The lock on the door is no more than a push button. I prop a chair under it. At least the noise will wake me up if someone breaks in.

Of course I can't sleep. With nothing to take the edge off I'm about ready to pull a nutty. The walls are so thin the party might as well be in here. Luckily for Mom, she just has to take out her hearing aids and she's sleeping like a baby.

Mac has to talk me down for half an hour tonight and I don't know how we'll afford the phone bill. But if ever I wanted a drink, I mean, was close to relapsing, this was the night. I feel sick inside all the time. Mom was so glamorous, so strong.

"I'm having crazy flashbacks again," I tell Mac.

"Don't go there, baby," he says, he knows.

"I can't help it, honey," I say, loving him hard, needing him badly.

"We can't do this, Soph," he says wearily.

"G'night sweetheart. I'm okay. Don't worry."

Oddly, Mom wakes up. She says she wants to see the magician's cape. I smile sadly at my mother before wrapping her coat around her shoulders and leading her outside. Together we look at the stars, blazing and twinkling like the stars on a magician's cape. Satisfied, she thanks me and goes back to bed.

Mom, what are you thinking? Then again, what am I thinking? Why is my mind playing tricks with me? The flashbacks are relentless, come without warning, and break my heart all over again.

TWENTY-SIX

I t had been a long drive from Wisconsin to Jack's home in New Hampshire, but in our high spirits the states flew by. Mac had driven back to Wisconsin for another week in late August to celebrate our engagement and follow through with Jack's plan for a week-long hike in the White Mountains of New Hampshire.

When we got on the road, Mac drove most of the way since Jack and I were pounding back Buds for most of the trip. Mac took it all in good humor, besides the old Buick was his baby.

Jack had insisted that whenever we stopped at rest areas, we would spread out hiking maps to study the trails and learn the topography of the White Mountains. Jack had bagged most of the four thousand footers and waxed poetically about the great views once you got above tree line. "Wait til you summit Mount Washington," he'd said. "It'll blow your mind."

Even though I wasn't an experienced hiker, I had strong legs and was in good shape. The hike would be strenuous but we would spend a night at Lakes of the Clouds, an Appalachian Mountain Club hut nestled in a col, high up on the mountain.

"We go up Tuckerman's Ravine, sleep at Lakes, summit in the morning, and then head down Lion's Head. The descent is tough on the knees, but it'll be easy to get back to the Buick." Jack knew the area well and was confident that this would be the way to go. Mac and I agreed.

"Just remember, it's serious up on Washington," he'd said. "No drinking the night before we climb, plenty of water, and gorp."

"Gorp?"

"Nuts, raisins and candy. Fuel."

Jack had pointed out the Tuckerman's Ravine trail on the map and traced his finger along every twist and turn so we could learn the route.

"When the lines are squished together, it means it's very steep."

Actually, the only place that looked really steep was the climb up the ravine. After that it was a straight shot across the top, then a left-hand turn over lichen-draped rocks where we would get our first view of the summit. Hang another left and we'd reach Lakes of the Clouds hut in time for dinner. "Dey serve mystery meat," Jack had laughed. "But you will be so hungry, you would eat a moose."

***

Jack's parents lived in a log cabin surrounded by tall pines. They ran out their front door the moment we pulled into their yard, thrilled to see Jack again and itching to meet me. The Thibodeaus were what you would expect, warm, hospitable and generous. His dad greeted us with the familiar wide-toothed grin, a strong handshake, and a gentle hug. His mother was quite pretty with jet black hair and hazel eyes that glowed almost yellow in the sunlight. She had cooked so much food in preparation for our visit that she'd filled her refrigerator and was storing treats in a cooler on the back porch.

Although they couldn't have been more gracious with

Mac and me, the Thibodeaus doted on their only child. They couldn't stop fussing over him, while piling extra heapings on his plate.

During dinner, the Thibodeaus occasionally slipped into Canuck French when they teased each other. Only his dad's elbowing and pointing in my direction gave clues as to what they were saying. Later, Jack told me that his dad and mom had observed that my wide hips were built for having children. We laughed and started a good-natured debate on how many children we each would like to have.

To this moment, I remember what Patrice Thibodeau served for dinner that evening. She had made mashed potatoes that were scooped in individual little baking dishes then crowned with a roasted chicken breast. Little cloves of garlic floated in a puddle of butter that moated around the potatoes. I had never tasted anything like it before or since. Years later, when Mac and I stopped to see her on our way to Bangor, she served the same meal, only this time the flavor was barely noticeable—a sad commentary on what had become of her life.

TWENTY-SEVEN

At three a.m. Mom awakens with a start. She jumps out of bed, looks in the mirror and screams at her reflection, "Who are you? What are you doing in my room? Get out!" When I try to hold her in my arms, she bites my hand, hard. Now I need a tetanus shot.

"Paul home!" I scream at my cell phone and wait as the voice recognition systems dials. I have to speak to Paul because if I tell Mac he'll want to rescue me or he'll call the kids and say awful things that only a blood relative can get away with.

No answer. I can't reach Paul. I don't care what time it is in el- lay. Izzy's awake, has just finished chanting and meditating.

"I'm scared and I'm mad. This motel is so seedy I swear I saw Charles Manson's twin brother walking around. I'm not sure I can keep this up."

"Calm down, Sophia. I would do anything to help you but Mahatma's shoulder has frozen up again and there's no way that she can spell me at the shop. Plus, the new owner wouldn't go along with it anyway."

"I'm losing it, Izzy. Just talk to me for awhile."

"Of course, honey. Do you know that we are thinking of you, praying, lighting candles and loving you?

"Who's we?"

"Mahatma and I. And dear Fiona called worried sick about you and Mom, and Paw-Paw loves you to death, girl."

"Is he lighting candles and burning incense?" It's odd how a sense of humor creeps in to save me every once in awhile.

"Probably not the candles because Alicia's allergic to anything with a scent. If you want me to send you some Valium, I can FedEx it."

"No thanks. I'll be fine."

"Well, let me know. Whatever you do, remember your sobriety."

Sweet, eh? Actually, she means well and is so far out there that I don't bother to scream. Instead, I am suddenly calmed.

"Thanks for your thoughts, the offer, nix on the Valium, Iz. Don't you take it either."

"I promise. I just have it for emergencies"

"Good. As for drinking, this is the most difficult thing I've done since going on the wagon. The triggers are unbelievable and I want a drink so badly I can scream, but just hearing your voice has calmed me down."

"Call anytime, honey."

"Okay, sorry if I interrupted anything."

Oh no, Mom's awake. She grabs the phone.

"Help, police!" she screams.

"Mom, Mom," Izzy yells. "It's me, Izzy. That's Sophia with you."

"Who?" Mom yells.

"*Sophia*," Izzy sounds frantic.

"Oh," Mom says, and then rests her head in the crook of my throbbing neck.

"I'm sorry dear; I don't know what's happening to me."

TWENTY-EIGHT

Maybe it's where the moon is; maybe she's totally disoriented sleeping in different rooms every night, whatever. All I know is that today she packs and unpacks her suitcase ten times. When I try to pull it away, she slaps me in the face. I cry so hard that I nearly lose my breath. Then suddenly she's my mom again, holding me, stroking me, and kissing me to make it better. It hurts so deep down inside and I can barely think about it, but what if this happens to me? I'd kill myself first.

***

At seven a.m. Tom calls. "Sorry for the short notice, but I have to tow it to the Ford dealership right now if the car is going to get looked at today." He's checked the car more closely and thinks the whole transmission needs to be replaced. Ford is the place to take it. Can he pick me up in a few minutes because I'll need to sign a repair contract with Ford?

Unfortunately, Mom is sound asleep. If I wake her, it will be over an hour to get her organized. If Tom and I are fast, I can be back before she awakens. I decide to chance it. I write her a note thinking that if she finds it, just reading it may slow her down fifteen minutes. I run down to the office and ask the man there to keep an eye out for her, giving the bare details of my predicament.

Tom arrives, car in tow, and we head into town. The

Ford place takes the car and confirms what Tom has told me. Confirming my worries, they don't have the parts they need. It's now 10:00 and I'm panicking about leaving Mom alone. What will she think when she wakes up and I'm gone?

When Tom drops me back at the motel, I run into the room, which isn't locked—and it's empty! In a panic, I rush down to the office, throw open the door and see Mom having her breakfast with the office manager. He has just told her something that she finds delightfully funny and she's giggling. She adores the attention and is behaving very coquettishly.

"Darlin, come meet my new beau." She smiles charmingly then insists that I take her coffee.

Oh, Mom.

Ford calls and says that they have to order even more parts. It's Friday afternoon and they won't get them in before Monday or Tuesday! I don't think I can handle this.

"Where is the car?"

"At the garage."

"Why? I want to leave," she repeats over and over.

"We can't leave until the car is fixed, Mom."

"Then leave it here," she says, dead serious.

"Don't tempt me," I say and I mean it.

To cap off the day she tells me there is a dog on her bed. "See, right there," she points.

"There's no dog there, Mom."

"Liar," she screams. "It has sharp teeth, make it go away."

Rather than argue, I yell at the bed. "Bad dog, go away, get out of here. Finally, I open the door and "push" it out.

I turn to her. "Okay?" She squints at me.

"You act crazy."

Just as I contemplate suicide, Paul calls.

"Soph, life has just heaved a shitload of lemons at you.

Make lemonade! I've called Sheraton, reserved a suite for you and Mom, put it on my credit card so you girls can have a little vacation."

"I wish I could fly through the phone line and kiss you."

Paul continues "Look at this as a holiday, Soph. Check into the Sheraton; eat in the dining room, order lobster, filet mignon, the works."

"You better not be fooling."

"I'd never do that, Soph. Listen, check out the IMAX theatre at the Science Museum. "

"That's a brilliant idea. I've been dying to see IMAX."

"Hold on for a second, I've got another call." I hear the BeeGees singing "Night Fever" as I stay on hold.

"I'm back and gotta run. Enjoy."

I'm almost giddy when I hang up. Of course, what Mom and I really need is a break from each other, but I'll try the Sheraton just the same.

The rental car company delivers a fairly nice car to the motel. Izzy calls as we're driving across town.

"Leave it to Paw-Paw!" she drools.

"He's a life saver," I say, meaning it.

"Soph, I know you won't believe this but I just asked for time off and my boss laughed. I tried, sis, I really did. I feel so helpless here."

My finger slips and I accidentally disconnect.

O-kaaaaaay.

TWENTY-NINE

We drive across town, spot the Sheraton, valet the car and charge it to our suite. Yeah baby!

Mom pronounces our suite, "royal" floats over to the window then tries to pry it open.

"The windows do not open, Mom". She's determined that they will.

When I try to explain to her the climate controlled concept, she replies, "That's ridiculous!" and continues to tug at the windows. For awhile I'm afraid we might have to change hotels again in search of fresh air. That probably would be hard in this soot-filled city!

To distract her from the windows, we have a blast at the Science Museum! There's an interactive area designed for children (of all ages) and it's just what we need. Lunch is great because we can eat outside by a huge man-made pond that has ducks and geese, and swans. Mom is thrilled. I have a little lump in my throat remembering taking her to the swan pond near my house, sitting amongst the lupine and listening to her recite Emily Dickinson's poetry by heart. For a moment, I'm lost in a warm, sweet memory pretending that this has all been a bad dream.

I'm beginning to see a pattern in Mom's eating that has me a bit concerned. Since we left home, every meal has bacon: BLT, grilled cheese and bacon, hamburger and bacon. Actually, those three items seem to be her repertoire. I try to suggest other things but she does a loud gagging routine so I give up.

While I'm on the subject of consuming, I'm really concerned about the effect alcohol has on her, especially in public. She's had cocktails at 5:00 since long before I was born. Actually, it's about the only constant she has. "Oh goodie, look dear, it's five after five," she says, licking her lips, eyebrows arched, and a twinkle in her eye. Plus, she expects me to join her!

"Mom, I know you don't remember, but I don't drink alcohol anymore. It makes me sick."

"I can't imagine why."

"Well, it just does and even a tiny drop will really make me so sick I would have to go to a hospital."

"Oh, my," she says. "Too bad. You'll have to stay home all the time."

Obviously, my mom enjoys the sociability of having cocktails with friends, neighbors and family, but with her declining health, I worry about her ability to drink. Her inability to express her thoughts becomes even more apparent, as do her rather shaky motor skills. Whenever I can manage it, I water down her drinks.

I decide to check out the IMAX theatre. Another hour or so can easily be passed there, or so I think. Who is the genius who invented IMAX? We get to our seats and Mom is excited as the theatre darkens. Then, WHOOSH! This humongous owl is flying straight for us! Yellow eyes piercing; giant wings flapping, claws dangling! Mom screams and screams! She ducks in her seat and hugs her knees. Mind you, she is not the only one startled in the theatre, just the only one that hasn't realized that the owl isn't real! She is terrified! Finally she sits back up and I stroke her arm and speak soothingly. I decide that as soon as she is calmed down we are outta here. Then she looks up and we are now soaring through the Grand Canyon, the walls of the canyon on either side, we're looking down at the Colorado River. "Whee!" she cries, rocking back and forth, grinning ear to ear.

I take a deep breath and relax a bit. Then we are up and out and flying over land. As we sweep down low, the tops of the trees tickling our toes, Mom gasps "ah" as we ascend again. She loves this. Her eyes are big and round with amazement. All signs of fear are gone. More birds. She loves the birds, pointing out their details in a loud voice. Fortunately, the surround-sound is very loud for effect and I don't think her talking is bothering anyone. She screams right along with me and everyone else in the audience as we jump off a cliff on *our* hang-glider. The rushes keep on coming and we are exhausted at the end of "our flying" experience. Afterwards, she finds it difficult to get her footing. As we leave the theatre arm in arm, she looks down at her watch and with a broadening smile declares it is 5:00! It has been a fun and delightful day.

Izzy calls on my cell phone and I tell her about our day.

"I know a lot of people in the movie business in el-lay. Let me get some copies of IMAX movies for Mom to watch in Wisconsin."

"She doesn't have a DVD player, Iz".

"I've got an extra one. I'll send it out today. It'll be at the house when you arrive."

"Uh, I don't know how to say this, Iz, but you need special equipment to watch an IMAX movie—like a theatre with a huge screen. Why don't you just get regular movies, like *The Sound of Music*? The DVD offer sounds great, though. "

"Okay." I hear Mahatma in the background—"Ohmmm".

On the way back from the theatre we pass a big park. I pull into a parking space and Mom and I watch children playing. I allow myself to drift into a daydream, remembering snapshots of Mom's childhood. In one of my favorites she was a pretty little girl in a party dress and Mary Jane shoes, blowing candles out on her sixth birthday cake. In another, she is barefoot, running across a lawn in Central Park blowing bubbles, being chased by little boys. I love that photo, but my favorite is the one of her at age 9 riding through Central Park dressed up as a cowgirl, replete with a western saddle, while the other little girls are properly dressed in habit, English style. There's Mom, sitting on her horse, Navajo, looking relaxed. One hand is holding the reins; the other is on her hip as she looks down at Grand-Dahlia who was afraid of horses.

THIRTY

As much as I'd love to sleep in, there's not a prayer. She's up and dressed and ready to go. So it's off to the petting zoo where Mom is totally enthralled. She delights not only in the animals, but engages every child she meets in conversation, including or should I say, especially, infants, with whom she shares in a special language all their own.

It's a toss up as to what is her favorite time. She was happy sitting by the pond and counting the ducks for several hours while I read my book. But she sure laughs hard and loud when the camel spits on me. Admittedly, it takes me awhile to see the humor, but her laughter is infectious.

Later, I check my email.

Fantastic! I've been hired to do the MacPhail wedding in August! I was hoping for it and now I have it. That's great news. What's funny is that they want a cake with Marzipan horses on it! Maybe I'll send a picture to Mom and she'll think the horses are dogs! Shame on me!

Mac has emailed me a very sexy card. He's a hottie, that old man of mine.

Just as I complete a gibberish conversation with Mom she surprises me with the secret ingredient to her Carbonara. Although I fantasized about keeping this secret to myself, I've decided to email the kids.

To: PVorelli@lawfrm.com
              IsabelaCam-aok@hotmail.com
From: Sophia@peisland.net
Subject: Secret ingredient

Mom finally told me her secret to the Carbonara sauce:
Add four red pepper flakes! YOU'RE WELCOME!
Saint Sophia, the good!

Paul sends back an instant message. He wants the entire Carbonara recipe. He's cooking for friends, blah blah and it's always been a showstopper. No kidding.

Of course I could email it to him but I'm feeling bratty now so I write it out and fax it to him from the Sheraton's business center.

CARBONARA A LA VORELLI

In a medium size pot:

2 T. olive oil

2 T. butter

1/2 lb. bacon

2 cloves fresh garlic (crushed)

4 red pepper flakes

Sauté the above over medium heat until the bacon is crispy.

When this mixture is slightly cool, add it to the following mixture:

In a small bowl—beat 3-4 eggs till frothy

Then add 1/4 c. parmesan cheese

Paw-Paw—This is our secret family recipe. If you share it, I'll shoot you.

"Why on earth would you add red pepper flakes?" Izzy asks later. Paul has already discussed this with her to determine if I've tried to trick him. He sends his emissary to do the detective work.

"Look, do what you want. Mom says she adds them and I tend to believe her, but maybe she means the saltimbocca. Why don't you just experiment?" I snap.

"You don't have to bite my head off, Sophia." Tinkle, tinkle, ohm, ohm.

"I can if I want to," I say, then take a deep breath and hang up.

THIRTY-ONE

F ord calls again. The part they are waiting for will be in on the 3:00 bus. They promise to have the car ready first thing Tuesday morning.

Mom doesn't take the news very well, nor do I. At lunch she insists on having a glass of wine and insists that I join her! I don't argue. There is no point in arguing with an Alzheimer's patient. Redirecting seems to work best. She really can't follow a logical thought process past one or two short sentences. Instead, I order a glass for myself and when she is distracted I dump it in a plant. That took more courage than I thought I had.

She has a new fixation today which is sad to watch, but keeps her occupied. She has brought with her a summer purse, shaped like a small basket. The top is made like a picnic basket where the two sides lift up. She opens up one side, empties it out into a pile, lifts the other side and does the same thing. Then she puts the first pile into the second side and vice versa, rearranging everything. Then she repeats the whole process over and over again. Clearly, we're both antsy to get going. We've had more than our fill of Southbury!

It warms me to know that despite the memory lapses, she still looks forward to the Derby. At the petting zoo she picked right up on the horse they had there and proclaimed it unfit for the Derby. Too fat! What else?? Not even overweight animals can escape her eagle eye. To hell with this.

THIRTY-TWO

Mac has an eagle eye, too. When we go fishing he can spot a school of fish just by a little ripple in the water. His vision is so sharp he can see the slightest movement from great distance. We sometimes joke that he would have made a great detective. There are no secrets when Mac is within a mile. We were sure he'd seen Jack and me making out on the porch that first time, in Grand-Dahlia's old cottage. Even though he was half a mile offshore.

Jack's kiss had come out of nowhere, yet we both knew it was coming. He wasn't the greatest kisser in the world—Mac is—but I still get a chill when I remember the soft envelope of Jack's lips covering mine. He'd blushed after kissing me, suddenly embarrassed. "Was it okay?" he'd asked sheepishly. I was so stunned by the depth of my response that the only thing to do was to crawl into his lap and return his kiss. Because we needed time to cool down, we held back, but we both knew where we were going.

"I'll tell him," Jack had said when we debated whether or not to hide our feelings from Mac. As it turned out, Mac couldn't have been happier.

"Outstanding," he'd said, wrapping his muscular arms around both of us.

We got rowdily drunk that night. The next morning, our heads pounded so badly that no one could eat, yet there were never three happier friends. Even though we swore that nothing would change in our relationship, it was out of our control. The chemistry between Jack and me was so strong that we found every excuse to bump up against each other. Mac sensed it and was generous enough to give us alone time. He made dozens of excuses, like going into town to buy food, getting lost in a hardware store, and taking the canoe out for hours at a time.

THIRTY-THREE

Thinking about our old birch bark canoe makes me remember the time Mom taught me the "J" stroke. I was seven or eight years old and had just recovered from the mumps. For my first outing after days in bed, Mom rewarded me with lessons on how to handle Grand-Dahlia's favorite canoe. "Straight in and curve like a "J" she instructed. I was good, did it on my first try. In minutes, we were paddling along the shoreline at a good speed, our J strokes in perfect harmony.

When our cruise had ended, we stowed our paddles and pulled the canoe onto the grassy shoreline. Mom was very excited. "You're a great first mate, Sophia. We'll take many trips together." Her expression was priceless, a mother and a pal rolled into one.

Lately, Mom's expression is like a blank piece of paper. There's nothing behind her eyes most of the time. Sometimes I see fear, but mostly I see a glass of water with nothing floating in it. Empty and scary. I fantasize about helping her die before she turns into a vegetable. I look at her and my skin crawls, my head hurts and my heart stabs me over and over. I don't want her to be my mother. I keep seeing Agatha Rose, the loveliest woman at the Red Cross ball, wearing a golden gown, dancing in my father's arms. Who is this withering flower? She looks like ashes of roses. I'm furious with you, God.

***

I'm also furious with my brother with his endless requests for recipes. It wouldn't be so bad if Mom could do email, but that's out of the question.

To:	Sophia@peisland.net
	IsabelaCam-aok@hotmail.com
From:	PVorelli@lawfrm.com

Subject: The fudge recipe

Soph sweetie, is there any chance you can ask Mom to give you the family fudge recipe? I'm feeling nostalgic and I've been telling my friends how when Mom was a little girl she would travel with her whole family from Chicago. You know how I love that story, Soph. How, they all took a train and the servants accompanied them to the family compound where they lived like kings and queens on the shores of Lake Michigan for the summer.

The part that blows everyone away is that there were cooks and all, so the family didn't have to do much— just make the fudge! No one can quite believe me, even though I tell him or her we all went there when we were babies.

Maybe the fudge recipe will prove it. What do you think? You're the best! Paw-Paw

Paul loves this story because it makes us sound rich as Rockefellers. We weren't and we aren't. I feel like screwing up the fudge recipe. In fact, I'm going to fax it instead of emailing it to him. The brat in me hopes he won't check his fax machine before he goes home.

Feeling guilty, I plan to leave him a voicemail at his office, but I call him instead. He surprises me by answering his phone. Of course I have to bitch at him a little bit. "Paul—you take the cake! Do you realize what I am going through? It wasn't enough that I had to write out the damn Carbonara recipe, now it's the fudge? What will it be tomorrow? The garlic chicken?"

"Listen tits," he teases, only daring to call me that when we are hundreds of miles apart, "the fudge is for Alicia, it's a special treat for her. "

"Okay big brother. I faxed you the recipe, but I warn you. It comes from an Alzheimer's patient. I can't remember it, but Mom swears this is it."

"Why didn't you email it to me?" he asks. I hear him take a sip of something. The ice cubes tingle on the glass.

"Because I'm feeling bitchy, that's why."

"Fair enough," he says sounding jolly. "Just remember who rescued you from the Bates Motel."

"Are you going to throw that in my face, asshole?"

He laughs, "But of course."

Peanut Butter Fudge—Grand-Dahlia and Grandpa's

2 c.	Sugar
2/3 c.	Milk
Dash	salt
2 c.	Peanut butter
1 c.	Marshmallow fluff

Mix sugar, milk and salt and cook 7 minutes or until a little of this mixture forms a soft ball when dropped into cold water. Remove the pan from the heat.
Add:
Peanut butter and fluff and beat it until it's creamy. Pour this mixture into a buttered 8-inch pan. Stick it in the fridge, and then cut into squares.

Your debt to me continues to grow,
Soph

The more I think about it the more I realize that we are so good at la-dee-dah-ing in my family. Oh yes, the fudge recipe. Sure, honey. It just kills me, that's all. I can see Mom in her taffeta and velvet dress, a big bow in her hair; everyone's darling, serving the fudge. This is the same woman who yesterday picked up scrambled eggs with her hands and rubbed them on her face.

BELLE HAVEN, WISCONSIN

THIRTY-FOUR

T he car is fixed and we're off! Better yet, we drive for two hours and we're in the United States! We cross the border in Sault Ste. Marie without a hitch, then drive across the damn tall bridge which is totally grated so you can see the water of Lake Huron below. Mom loves it, sticks her head out the window and hangs out her tongue like a dog while I grip the steering wheel and curse the damn bridge. By the time I reach the opposite side, I'm shaking. Now it's across the Upper Peninsula and voila, Wisconsin.

The sky is robin's egg blue, startling against the deep green of the pine trees. I stop to stretch and inhale the tingling heavy scent of pine. There's a scratching sound not far from where I've squatted to pee. It could be a deer; then again it could be a bear so I high tail it back to the car. Despite the nip in the air, there's a distinct promise of spring.

***

We arrive in Belle Haven and I'm reminded that I really love it here. I can't wait to get to Mom's rambling house with its wonderful glassed-in side porch. Papa had added the second floor bedrooms, converting the attic into a dormered suite for themselves. The grownups wanted their privacy from their wild brood.

When I pull into the driveway, Mom chirps in the direction of the birdhouse. "Let me out," she yells.

"Yes, indeedy," I answer, hoping that her familiar surroundings will have a positive effect.

I climb the front steps, totally unprepared for what greets me after turning the key in the lock.

The smell is overwhelming. Rotting food, cat pee, old people smell. The first thing I notice is the stained carpeting, then the furniture. Her antique Louis XIV chairs are ripped to shreds by sharp cat claws; the stuffing has oozed out of the sofa. Her two winged-backed chairs are covered with ratty old towels to hide the destruction that Peekay has caused.

My first thought is that Mom had left the poor cat trapped in here when she left, but then I remember that Nelly said she has Peekay in her care. No small favor if Mom's house is any indication. The drapes are tattered and coated with layers of cat hair. Everything is covered in cat hair! For the first time, I'm glad that Mac couldn't make the trip. Most of the cat smell originates from an overflowing litter box, which takes me several attempts to empty before I can do it without gagging.

Dust layers everything and I don't mean a few weeks' absence kind of dust. Clutter is everywhere. I open the fridge. More gagging. The kitchen cabinets house bug-infested food and cans that have expiration dates long ago passed. I don't dwell too long on thoughts of what she had been eating over the last few months.

I try to blank out what I'm seeing and think about how we lived in Barcelona. Our house was run like a palace. In her broken Spanish, Mom could manage barefoot maids just out of the mountains. She could cajole even the laziest girl to work hard and take pride in it. The house would shine; you could eat off the floors. And the meals were unbelievable. I remember when she would stand in the kitchen with Magdalena, our cook, jabbering away in Spanglish, watching her prepare paella and garlic soup, tasting, stirring and trying new spices while downing margaritas, mojitas, sangria—and that was before dinner! The rest of the night she wanted her bourbon. Out of respect to her Louisville roots, she'd say. I don't think I was more than fifteen before she invited me to join her.

THIRTY-FIVE

oor Nelly. Mom has called her seven times to be sure she's coming over. But that's not all. She has a 900 number taped to the wall near the phone. For the hell of it, I punch in the numbers. It's a phone sex line.

"Mac, you won't believe this," I say to my patient husband who has just called to check on our arrival.

"Try me, Chiquita," he says using that sexy voice of his.

"I think she's been calling a phone sex line."

"Way to go, Aggie Ro," he laughs.

"This is serious, honey," I persist.

"Okay, baby, I'll fly out to Wisconsin. Sounds like you need me."

I'm tempted by his offer, but with the cat hair everywhere, he wouldn't be able to walk through the door without a serious risk to his health.

"Love you for offering, though," I say, grateful to him, as always.

***

As I work my way from room to room, Mom follows watching my every move. It's as if she thinks I'm going to steal something. She eyes me and struggles to say, "Last time you took my Limoges ash—- ." I want to argue back, I'm so insulted. But I'm too tired and strung out.

Finally I'm able to sneak off to the porch to call Paul from my cell phone. Thank God I catch him as he's about to leave for court. For once he doesn't argue with me.

"It's catshit everywhere," I moan.

"Thanks for making me sick to my stomach. Are you sure you're not exaggerating?"

"If you accuse me of that one more time—"

"Sorry. Just call in a cleaning service and send me the bill.

"Paul, can't you please get out here now?" There's tightness in my chest. I'm falling apart and need his presence in the flesh.

He clears his throat; I hear horns beeping and someone hawking Celtics tickets in the background. "I'm way behind, Soph. My ass is parked here until the case is over," he says sounding every bit the Boston barrister, even his 'A's' have flattened.

Forget it. I run for the Yellow Pages and score on the first number. They aren't too busy this time of year. They can be here in an hour and stay for as long as it takes. Yeah, baby. Of course I have to get Mom out of the house and distract her for hours, but that shouldn't be hard. We can hit the swan pond, the beauty parlor and the Flying Fools Lodge, her favorite spot for a toddy and dinner. That should be long enough. Finally, for the first time since our trip began, I feel like I'm taking control.

I even laugh when Paul calls back on my cell phone. "Don't go so batshit over catshit," he says, trying to be serious. Then he laughs that special Paul machine gun staccato laugh that he's had since he was a little boy, the same laugh that got him thrown out of Sunday School more times than I can count.

I'm warmed by the memories of our youth, until the tears flood without warning.

***

In my haste to get the house cleaned I almost forgot why we had to stop in Wisconsin. One glance to its usual resting place and I speed dial my husband.

"Good news, honey! The book is here, right on the coffee table and in good shape. Thank God for small favors!"

Mac cheers by making some ungodly sound he learned on the Island, a cross between my moose imitation and a yodel. Then he gets serious. "Everything's going to be all right, baby, so please try to relax and maybe even enjoy being in Belle Haven. Take Aggie to the drug store and suck down one of those chocolate ice cream sodas, okay?"

"See, this is why I love you, Mac."

"Is that the only reason?"

"Yeah," I joke.

"Oh yeah? Then maybe I need to fly out there, start at your toes, and remind you of a thing or two."

"Silly Mac, I love you more than anything in this world," I say feeling butterflies in my stomach and a warm ache beginning.

"You better, babe, 'cause you're stuck with me."

Thank God, I tell myself.

THIRTY-SIX

Paul calls during noon recess from court. He's coming, I just know it.

"Sophia honey, listen. This is really important to me. I can't bear the thought of what you've told me. And to be honest, sometimes I filter what you tell me."

"You do what?" The mellow mood that Mac put me in dissolves.

"I filter because you've always had this competition thing with Mom." He sounds apologetic and patronizing, not what I need today. I chew on my lip.

"You're crazy, you know that?"

"No, look, don't get me wrong. I think it comes from you being oldest. After all, you were the uber-big sister, always so helpful, the first to straighten my tie when we went to church. Mommy's little helper."

"Did you say goober-sister?"

"Uber-sister. You know, the best, top of the heap."

"Am I talking to Paul Vorelli or F. Lee Bailey?"

"That's very good, except Lee was disbarred in Florida. Seriously, Soph, I can't stand the way you talk about Mom. In my mind she's still the fluffernutter queen, the sweet-faced, twinkle-eyed mummy who slid under the covers with me when she read me a bedtime story."

"I know Paul, I wish."

He doesn't hear me, just rambles along. "She came to every one of my football games, even when she was just a week out of gall bladder surgery."

"I know honey. It's horrible." What else can I do but suffer along with him? I think that maybe it's starting to get through to him. It's like slowly peeling an onion.

"Alicia has always liked Mom, even when she doesn't like me," he continues. "I remember when I brought Alicia home to meet Mom and Papa. Mom was wearing black slacks, a white tailored shirt with her black cashmere sweater tied over her shoulders. Alicia described her outfit ad infinitum, citing it as the ultimate in good taste and style."

"Alicia's description is perfect, bro. Her good taste is what makes her stand out in a crowd."

"Right. So what you are describing is someone who is on the edge of dementia, who can't even match her shoes, who's rude and nasty and..."

"And going to get worse, Paul, much worse."

THIRTY-SEVEN

I 've taken everything that's salvageable to the dry cleaners. They're going to attempt to mend the drapes, which is certainly better than having to replace them. I had to throw out the teakettle and the toaster; both had been badly burned. The cleaning crew has scrubbed the house from top to bottom, cabinets and fridge, cleaned and polished. What a relief.

I don't have the heart to tell the kids how her bedroom smells. Her mattress should be thrown out. To make maters worse, the damn cat has pissed on her blankets (probably in her absence) and Mom keeps spraying perfume. I gag a lot and fantasize about killing the cat, but stop short because of what it would do to Mom.

As we take our coffee on the porch, Mom seems more relaxed. Peekay hasn't stopped purring since we got him back; he and Mom just sit in the sun and purr together. He is big and fat, probably weighs 25 pounds. I'm afraid he gets fed more than she does! I'm trying to stop him from further destroying the furniture, but I know when I'm licked. He has ruled this house for a long time and he doesn't have to listen to me. Besides, every time I yell at him, Mom tells me to let him alone, he is so cute! Peekay and I are not very fond of each other; he dislikes me for my interfering and I dislike him because he is a destructive pain in the neck. However, we have reached some sort of unspoken truce for Mom's sake.

***

Tonight, I tuck Mom into a nice, fresh bed. As she lies there propped on pillows, her teeth in the glass next to her bed, she looks as innocent as a child. I remember lying there, sick with the measles and sad to be in bed. That was when she taught me the Japanese Lullaby. "Would you like to hear it, Mom?" I ask.

"Oh goodie", she replies.

> *Sleep, little pigeon, and fold your wings,—*
> *Little blue pigeon with velvet eyes;*
> *Sleep to the singing of mother-bird winging—*
> *Swinging the nest where her little one lies.*

Remarkably, Mom joins in; stumbling over some words, forgetting others, but her long-term memory still is strong. Together, we continue:

> *Away out yonder I see a star,—*
> *Silvery star with a tinkling song;*
> *To the soft dew falling I hear it calling—*
> *Calling and tinkling the night along*
>
> *In through the window a moonbeam comes,—*
> *Little gold moonbeam with misty wings;*
> *All silently creeping, it asks, "Is she sleeping—*
> *Sleeping and dreaming while mother sings?"*

KENTUCKY RAIN

Up from the sea there floats the sob
Of the waves that are breaking upon the shore,
As though they were groaning in anguish, and
moaning—
Bemoaning the ship that shall come no more.

But sleep, little pigeon, and fold your wings,—
Little blue pigeon with mournful eyes;
Am I not singing?—See I am swinging—
Swinging the nest where my darling lies.—
Eugene Field

Much later, when it's impossible for me to sleep, I walk from room to room, replaying scenes from my childhood. This house is the glue that has held us all together. I can't imagine the pain of losing it.

THIRTY-EIGHT

Today, I try to determine our next steps. It is now abundantly clear that Mom can no longer live without supervision. If I hadn't witnessed the mess of the house first-hand I might be fooled into thinking she's doing pretty well, but when I step out of the shower, the thought of her independent living washes away. It takes me a few seconds to realize that she's called the 900 number and is giggling like a little girl. "You naughty boy," she says, over and over. I wrap a towel around me and drip over to her.

"Hang up the phone, Mom, it costs a lot of money to speak to that person."

"No!" she says, sticks out her tongue and snatches my towel, leaving me bare-naked and shivering. I give up and stomp from the room. When I return, she's sitting on the couch hugging a pillow rocking back and forth, crying. "Help me, someone help me".

God, how I hate hearing those words!

When she takes her nap, I climb the attic stairs for no good reason other than I'm going through the entire house. I guess in the back of my mind I know that we'll have to sell it sooner rather than later.

In the gentle hue of the fading light coming in from the dormer windows, I'm moved by what I see. Lying across the old brass bed are some of our family's long discarded outfits. My tiny blue sweater with the yellow-billed duck appliqué rests above matching blue and yellow trousers; Izzy's tie-dyed t-shirt is next to Paul's football sweater. If that isn't enough to make me melancholy, my next discovery rips my heart out. Mom has taken her silver strapless Scaasi gown, stuffed it with tissue to fill it out so it looks like there's a body in it, then laid it on the floor next to Izzy's giant teddy bear which now wears Papa's tuxedo with sleeves and pants folded under. A dried rose on a long withered stem lies at the bear's feet.

I can picture her up here daydreaming of dancing with Papa. Oh, that poor sweet lady.

"Mac," I cry, when I describe it to him.

"You shouldn't be sad," he says. "She's had a great life, your father and mother were mad for each other, and you have to believe that when she did this she had a smile on her face just remembering."

"God, I hope so."

"And honey, I hope that when I'm gone, you'll smile every time you think of the fun we've had. Start smiling right now, Sophia. It's all part of living. Look at the good side, sweetheart."

THIRTY-NINE

Thank God that Mom had been coherent enough to carry her passport when she flew to the Island, or she never would have been allowed on an airplane. I've been looking for Mom's wallet since we arrived. Before she came to the Island, Nelly had someone from Public Health come over to assess her and Mom didn't trust her. Her wallet has been missing ever since. I keep hoping she'll remember where she stashed it. Every once in awhile she asks if I've seen it or taken it and I keep asking her if she remembers where it might be, but so far no luck.

I open up Mom's desk today and though nothing should be a surprise any more, I am shocked at the state of her financial affairs, amazed that we have electric and phone service. I'm guessing that this is one of the benefits of living in a small town. Anyway, I have far too much to deal with, so I pay the more immediate bills, or should I say try to get Mom to sign some checks. This is no small task.

"Stay out of my business!" she yells. "I've paid all my bills and no one is getting a penny more." She's upset and confused and I feel like a bully. She's crying. I'm crying. I can't imagine how it must feel to be losing your mind and control of your life. Isn't *she* supposed to be the person who's strong and steady, the one who was always grounded and could be relied upon? Mom was the person I could turn to with *my* financial problems and now *she can't remember how to sign a check.*

When the fight ends and the time comes to hug and say we're sorry, she doesn't reach out to me. Instead, she retreats to some far off place. In spite of the moments where she seems to be her old self, for the most part she's suspended in a disintegrating spider web. She's not depressed; at least I don't think so, but she's not happy either. She doesn't appear to be bored, nor is she interested in anything for very long. So I hug myself. She's already moving on in her mind and I'm left with my guilt and a feeble promise to myself to be a better daughter, a stronger person and more understanding.

***

A few hours later she kicks me. When I jump away, she loses her balance and falls. When I try to help her get up she scrambles away screaming, "Stop, thief!" I have to call Nelly to get help in calming her down. When Nelly arrives Mom's still agitated. She takes a handful of Nelly's hair and begins to pull. Nelly is smarter than I am so she reaches up and pulls Mom's hair. Miraculously, this stops everything and calms her down.

"Did you come for tea?" she asks Nelly, as if nothing has happened.

"No, I've come to take you for a walk," Nelly answers, nodding at me.

"I'll just get my purse," Mom says and off they go. I leave the house, too and buy a pack of cigarettes, my first in fifteen years. One puff and a phone call to my sponsor and I toss the pack. Instead, to busy my hands, I check my email.

To:<u>Sophia@peisland.net</u>

From: <u>IsabelaCam-aok@hotmail.com</u>

Subject: I honor you

Sophia—Remember what Emily Dickinson said, "We never know how high we are until we are called to rise; and then, if we are true to plan, our statures touch the skies". You really are the sugar plum fairy.

I love you,

Izzy

Well Izzy, this is one sugar plum fairy that is dying for a scotch!

FORTY

As I'm about to leave her winter coat with the pile I've made to take to the homeless shelter, I find a letter in the pocket. An alarm goes off in my brain. I set the note off to the side for a few minutes before reading it, and then I get up my nerve. There's no date on the note but it seems old. Even though the paper has taken on a suede-ish feel, the words are painfully clear.

Although I try to type the letter into an email, my hands shake too much. Nelly agrees to stay with her while I run to the drugstore where there's a fax machine. I race numbly into town, ice-cold, feelings shut down. Before faxing, I call the kids to warn them. The letter is dated almost two years ago.

Dear Children:

Although I am clearly losing my mind I still think clearly once in awhile. This is one of those times. Although you may think I am writing fiction, my dear friend Nelly will verify that I am currently of sound mind.

I have just come from the doctor's office and, like my father before me; I have the beginning stages of Alzheimer's disease. This is a nuisance, quite bothersome and frightening. What I hate most about it is that I can no longer finish the New York Times crossword puzzle. On the other hand, what I like most about it is that I feel closer with your father and my parents. We have great times together. Why just the other night I had a very clear dream about the time Papa and I went to the Villa d'Este, how we tangoed until the wee hours of the morning and walked hand in hand in the moonlight. Your father was an exquisite man—a wonderful husband, devoted friend and very romantic. I've had it all, having had him in my life.

While I am still able to focus I want to tell you how proud I am of all of you. No mother could ask for better children. Certainly you were spirited, and perhaps the police visited me a little too often, but when the chips were down, you've all been there for your father and me. We love you dearly— warts and all.

Now I have some apologies to make. Paul, you're the youngest, I'll start with you. I want to apologize to you for giving you the workaholic genes in our family. They certainly didn't come from your father and me, but my father was a maniac, a demon of a worker, even though he was a shrewd Wall Street lawyer who made a good living and could have had a much more relaxed life. You have something else of him in you, too—your wandering eye. Don't deny it, my lamb chop, mothers know these things. Perhaps you can address these weaknesses and fix them before they get the best of you. If you want to do something for me, that's what I ask. To thine own self be true, Darlin Paul. Embrace your life, take time for yourself, savor the joy in your marriage, or leave Alicia and find someone with whom you can find true happiness. And one more request. Make peace with Sophia. Ever since the accident, the two of you have butted heads and I don't know why. It's time for forgiveness for whatever it is that makes you two so angry with one another.

Isabela, my little girl. That was always the problem, wasn't it? Here you were, my baby, prettiest of my children, pampered and spoiled until your father intervened. I want to apologize to you for making you believe I would never accept the fact that you are gay. I just want you to know that I accept your life choice and I hope you will bring your girlfriend to visit me soon. I also want to apologize to you for giving you my addiction genes. It's true that I've been an alcoholic since college and you know that it runs in families. Your father was probably an alcoholic, too, although both of us functioned quite well, or so it seemed. Izzy, I want you to stop living in the past and live for each day. I truly believe that if you go to your meetings and call your sponsor every day you will beat this thing. You have to, my sweet lamb, so I won't have to worry about you.

Sophia mia—. My firstborn, my rock. You have been more wonderful to me than any mother could ever hope for. Ever since you were a tiny girl, you always seemed to watch out for me. I know sometimes you are misunderstood, but your father and I always marveled how you paid attention to detail, dotting every "i" and crossing every "t". Probably you've inherited this from your father's side—certainly great sculptors carried this gene which was passed along to you—just look at those marvelous cakes you dream up.

I want you to know how proud I am of you. I worried so much after you came home from New Hampshire. How I longed to take your heartache and pain and carry it for you. When we nearly lost you I wanted to die. But look at you now, a beautiful life with darling Mac, a wonderful home, dear friends. I beg of you, relax and smell your wonderful flowers and before I die, please fix things with your brother. You both suffered a terrible loss, darling.

One more thing. I can see you in my dreams tossing and turning night after night worrying about what's going to become of me. If you ask me to move to that godforsaken land you call home one more time I'll scream. On the other hand, I'd rather be dead than go to a nursing home. Let me just say that when the time comes, I want all my babies to get together and figure out a way for me to stay in my home, here in Wisconsin.

Having watched my father drift away with this disease, I know what's in store for me. That's why it's important that I tell you while I am still quick with my pen that I love each of you more than life itself. I have had the most wonderful life, married the most magnificent man, been absolutely delighted with my role as a mother and I think I've had more fun than most women I know.

Hopefully, they will find a cure before you get to be my age. It is this thought that hangs heavy on my heart today. But, alas, I shall call each of you, listen to your tinkling laughter and make myself nice toddy before going to bed, dreaming of my Darlins.

Always my love,

Mom

When I return and Nelly leaves, I read her letter again, finally allowing myself to feel, knowing that my heart has cracked right down the middle. When I find the courage to face Mom, I find her asleep in the den.

I study the woman in the chair. "Please be kind to her God," I say softly. Her hair catches the rays of the sun dropping in the west. As I watch her sleep I see how peaceful she is. I fold the letter and slide it into my pocket. I just need to hold her hand. I wish I could talk to her, not the woman in the chair, but the mother who wrote the beautiful letter. She is sleeping with Peekay on her lap and a photograph of Papa on the table next to her chair. I want to wake her up and have my old Mom open her eyes. I want her to say "April fool" and dab away my tears. But she's so far away now that it's impossible to know what she understands. Still I must try. I get down on the floor and press my head next to her lap robe.

She stirs and I think she's awakened, but I'm mistaken. It's Peekay's foot on my head that I feel.

FORTY-ONE

Today the air sparkles outside, "like a glass of champagne", as Mom used to say. I've never forgotten that phrase and today I'm feeling particularly melancholy because there's a kind of fizz in the air. The wind sweeping down from Canada carries the Arctic chill, but the sun is so warm I can taste it. I inhale several times, smiling as I draw each breath deeper and deeper into my lungs, until I feel lightheaded and woozy.

Mom's letter has silenced my siblings. They've sent an amazingly fragrant gardenia plant as a sign of their love, a short note to Mom and me, and not a word about its contents. Actually, that's good. I'm not ready to climb that mountain any time soon.

***

Nelly asked me to call her when Mom takes her nap. She arrives with her blueberry cake and a thermos of coffee. Before she begins, Nelly reaches into her flowered blouse and adjusts her flesh-colored bra strap.

"These puppies are getting too heavy for me to lug around," she says, shifting the heft of her breasts until she's comfortable.

I shamelessly dive into the delicious treat while Nelly shifts around in her chair.

"I don't think your Mom should live alone any more."

This is obvious, but hearing it from my mom's dear friend makes it gong like a death knell.

"I agree, Nell, but I'm having trouble with Paul and Izzy over this. Can you give me some ammunition?"

Nelly smoothes her dress, shifts her breasts again and pushes at her cuticles.

"You know when you get to be my age you sleep less and less," she begins." Well, one morning I heard a banging at my door around 4 am. It was your Mom."

"At four in the morning!"

"Yes. And she was stark naked."

I cover my face, shake my head and begin to laugh like a crazy person.

"It's not funny, Sophia," Nelly admonishes. She reaches over to wipe a crumb from my face and then she joins me in a fit of laughter.

When I can control myself, I ask Nelly why she hadn't called me immediately.

"I didn't want to embarrass Aggie. I knew you'd find out sooner or later. I just didn't want to be the one to break the news."

"Ah."

***

After polishing off her second slice of cake and refilling my coffee cup, Nelly leaves. I sit there worried about money. If we need to take care of Mom the way I think we will it's going to take more moolah than I think she's got socked away. Peekay rubs his body against my leg. He looks up at me with that face of his and meows, as if he is trying to tell me that he's glad I know. I wish I didn't.

FORTY-TWO

I have a sudden urge to flip over Grand Dahlia's Persian rug that covers most of the dining room floor. I turn the edge of the rug over, splay my fingers, and turn my hand over twice, measuring carefully. Yep, there is my little secret. In the heat of Presley-mania I had printed a message with an indelible pen on the back of the rug. I decide to let the cat out of the bag.

"Look, Mom" I say, inviting her to bend down and inspect my handiwork."

She crouches and squints, studies it hard then laughs.

"It says I love elves" she chuckles.

"No, Mom, it says I love ELVIS,"

"You do?" Her eyes grow wide.

"No, I did. This is almost thirty years old."

She shrugs and gets up. "I love elves too, but I wouldn't write it on a carpet."

Instead of continuing the conversation, I'll make my tenth attempt to give her a bath. It's been random showers ever since she came to PEI.

I 've also been trying to get her to change out of the same old sweater that she continues to wear day after day. Every time I suggest she take it off and let me wash it she wraps her arms around herself and says, "No, no, Frederick gave this to me." Frederick! Her first boyfriend over fifty years ago! I'd love to know what is going on in her mind!

***

I'm finally able to convince her that it's splish splash time when I hand her a big fluffy hot-from-the-dryer towel. I've already run a few inches of warm water in the tub and added bubble bath. She rubs her face in the warmth of the towel.

"Ooooh," she moans.

"I'll get another one ready for you for when you get out of the water."

"Goodie."

She goes straight to the bathroom and gets undressed. As I help her into the tub, I notice what good shape her body is in even though she's very thin. It seems that only her mind is sagging, and quickly at that. Peekay watches skeptically as I lower Mom into the water. He still doesn't trust me.

She's frightened of falling at first and seems to have other fears of the water that escape me. Once she is in the water, though, it's an entirely different story. She is a child again, sliding down into the water until only her nose and eyes peek out above the bubbles. Then she closes her eyes, her shoulders droop and I can see her whole body relax. I sit quietly on the floor next to the tub and stay with her for reassurance. After a bit, she opens her eyes, gently blows the bubbles and giggles. She does it again and again. Then, that impish look comes into her eyes, her eyebrows arch, arm pulls back and the next thing I know I'm covered in soapy water. She splashes me again and again and laughs. I wiggle down the wet floor to the other end of the tub and get into fighting position and the next thing we know we're in a full-fledged water-fight. Peekay is having none of it and makes a dash for the door. He's never going to trust me now.

Since her hair is wet, she lets me wash it, and once again I'm struck by our role reversal. She holds up the washcloth to protect her eyes from the soapy water while I wash her hair, daughter acting as mother, and mother becoming daughter.

After her bath she announces, "I'll do this," marching toward the laundry with her towels and clothing. Then she stands there, not knowing how to turn it on. So I put in the soap and fabric softener and pushed the right buttons. Still, she keeps opening the lid, which stops the cycle. She repeats this seven times...today.

***

Later, Izzy and I have a long talk.

"I love remembering Mom taking her baths. When we were in Spain I used to think she was like a matador dressing for the bullfight."

"It's funny," I say. "I barely have time to step into the shower and Mom could spend the whole afternoon pampering for the evening."

"You used to roll her hair in the back for her."

"You remember that?" I ask, very surprised. Izzy was a tiny girl when we lived in Barcelona.

"Of course I do." I can see her now under her hair dryer, with the plastic hat like a shower cap with a hose sticking out of it.

I laugh remembering that contraption. Mom looked so funny sitting under her dryer with the hot air poofing it up, but she was dead serious as she sat there drying, while giving herself a pedicure and manicure. Izzy is quiet for a moment. I hear her sip some liquid.

"Soph?"

"What?"

"Yesterday I noticed my reflection in a storefront window. I look like a flaky old hippie with wild hair and no makeup.

Then I thought of Mom and realized that she'd never go out looking like this."

Izzy's starting to sniffle, the sobs are coming.

"Know what I did? I bought a bottle of Shalimar for myself, just so I could smell her and remember..."

"Sweetie," I say. "I wish you were here with me, just so we could be together, you know?"

"I know me too. But you know what, Soph? No matter which she said in that letter, I think it kills her that she has a dyke for a daughter."

FORTY-THREE

Bingo! I find Mom's wallet in the bottom of the Grandfather clock! She must have opened up the glass door and tossed it in. I'm not sure what made me look there, except I'd run out of all reasonable and some not so reasonable places to search. I just don't understand what's going on in her head.

The clock is a beauty, bought in Europe during one of Papa's job rotations. The American dollar was strong enough to pay for rentals on wonderful villas and there was always a staff to help her out. It was a sweet life for them, made even better because they had a real thing for each other. He called her, "cara". And she called him "sugar pie". The memory brings a smile to my face—which disappears a minute later. My mother was an amazing cook, very fussy about everything that went in our mouths. So you can imagine how I felt when I saw her sit down to a can of cat food!

Izzy and Paul call just as I close my eyes. This time it's Izzy who has instituted the call and she's very proud of herself.

She says, "You know that Mahatma is a holistic healer, very connected spiritually to Mom through me. She's been beaming healing thoughts Mom's way."

"Not now," I groan. "I've had a stomach ache for an hour and you're making me nauseous."

Izzy ignores me. "Mahatma says that maybe Mom could be made a lot better with some gingko bilboa. It's worked wonders for old folks, even reversed dementia. And she wants Mom to take up Tai Chi. Isn't it worth a try?" Izzy sounds sweet and caring. Here's how Paul sounds.

"With all due respect, Izzy, tell your friend Mahatma to stop filling your head with ludicrous solutions. Ask her to fax me a copy of her medical degree." Ah yes, way to go Paul.

Izzy shrills, "Did it ever occur to you that there are things in the universe we know little or nothing about? Try thinking out of the box, as you yuppies like to say."

I hang up and leave the receiver off the hook.

It occurs to me that Mom often doesn't remember my name. This becomes more obvious tonight, when Nelly arrives for Mom's birthday dinner. Mom tries to introduce us and can't remember my name, not to mention the fact that Nelly and I have known each other for years.

As dinner progresses, it gets pretty interesting. If you didn't know Mom or our family you'd consider her to be a perfect hostess delighting her guests with a few family anecdotes. However, since I do happen to know our family, I find it remarkable to listen to stories about people I have never heard of. She speaks of grandchildren that don't exist, kids on college football teams, when no one is in college. Her stories are funny and quite vivid; unfortunately these people only exist in her mind. Then again, I wonder if these are the people she wished her children to be, or people from her past that she has reborn into her present life. Or maybe I just analyze too much and should let it go to just making conversation. After all, it is Nelly, who has known us forever and loves Mom like her own sister.

Tonight, as it is a birthday celebration, it is hard to try and talk Mom out of a bottle of wine with dinner following cocktails. I have been sucking down Virgin Mary's like no tomorrow. Then it's time to open presents.

Izzy sent vitamins, gingko bilbao from Mahatma, and a crystal, which Mom loves. Paul sent a tapestry cat lap robe that she keeps holding to her cheek and purring, Mac and I bought her a coffee table size book with fabulous photographs of the cats that live in Rome's Coliseum. However, Nelly takes the cake with her present—a photo of Frank Sinatra upon which Nelly has written a love note to Mom and forged his autograph! We play Sinatra records and Mom asks me to dance, snuggling up cheek-to-cheek. Help me, Jesus!

FORTY-FOUR

Mom has a bad day today. Maybe it was too much alcohol last night. After her breakfast, she walks around the living room looking at all the family photos on the walls and tables. Her eyes are wide and she is visibly upset.

"I don't know these people, why they look at me?" she asks. A chill runs down my spine.

"What people, Mom?"

"These people," she says pointing from one family photograph to another. Then, coming to a photo of Izzy and Paul as toddlers, she smiles and says, "Well, I know these two little chicks." But I see the unsettled look in her eyes as she looks over at the last photograph that was taken when we adult children were together. She has no idea who we are.

"I don't want strangers looking at me. Get them out of my house." She turns over all the ones on the tables and desk. "I don't know these people," she keeps repeating.

At first I am stunned and a little frightened. As she keeps talking, I realize that she is relating to our baby photos and it begins to make some sense. Mom adores children and always has. The photos that she allows to remain on the walls and around the house are all of when we were young children. Still, it is eerie to watch her look at photos of Papa and not recognize him. Needless to say, we remove all the photos of "strangers" and she seems content.

147

Just as I put my feet up, Mom stomps up to me and accuses me of stealing her book. Rather, she says, "That woman in the kitchen stole it".

Of course, *I* am that woman.

A few minutes later, Chief Halvorsen arrives. It seems Mom called the cops on me, accusing me of stealing from her. I don't have much explaining to do, thankfully. Apparently, they all know Mom in Belle Haven, but the scene she puts on is one for the books.

I fully expect her to shriek, "Stop, thief. Arrest her."

Naw.

Evidently, she has no memory of calling the police, clueless as to why they've come. Instead, she mistakes Halvorsen's uniform for a World

War II Army Air Corp uniform. So what does she do? She sings to him, knowing about three-quarters of the words to "Wild Blue Yonder". God love Halvorsen; he returns her salute and marches out the door.

I'm sorry, I can't stop laughing. I almost wet myself as she stands there holding her salute in her ancient Vassar sweatshirt and older still Pendleton wool pants with Fiona's old Mickey Mouse ears perched cockeyed on her head. When she realizes I'm laughing at her she sticks out her tongue, then gives me a Bronx salute! Where did she ever learn that?

***

Later, I tuck her in for a nap so I can get some things together for our trip. After awhile I realize that the house is extremely quiet. I call out to Mom. No answer. Knowing full well that she doesn't have her hearing aids in, it is really pointless to continue calling. Then I realize that Peekay, too, is among the missing. A small twinge of panic begins to surface.

I run to the front door and fly outside and there is Mom, sitting on the front porch in her rocker, cuddling Peekay and smiling up at me.

"Hi, Darlin," she says. Relief floods through me. I start to smile back until I realize that behind Peekay, one of Mom's breasts is staring at me. She is sitting there naked from the waist up. All of a sudden I am extremely grateful for the size of this fat cat that is hiding most of my mother's nakedness.

"Mom, what are you doing?" Dumb question!

"Sitting on the porch, dear."

Deep breath. "Mom, you don't have your sweater on."

"No, I was warm. I took it off." Logical answer. I'm trying to stay calm

I scan the neighborhood for anyone who might be passing by.

"OK, well, um, you can't sit on the front porch without something on."

"I most certainly can. It's my house."

"Yes, it is your house, but it is cold out."

"I'm warm."

She kisses Peekay's head. I beam my thoughts at the cat. Please, please, Peekay don't move. I go inside and get her a blouse and come back out. Peekay is still in position. Tuna for the fat shit tonight, I think.

"Here, Mom," I say, trying a fresh approach, in what I hope is a cheerful voice. "Put this on, it's lighter than your sweater."

She says nothing, continues to stroke Peekay. Then I add, "You sure don't want to catch a cold before we get to the Derby." Bingo! She takes the bait. As if on cue, Peekay does one last head rub on her chin and jumps down. I quickly step forward and help her into the blouse. Thank God for Peekay.

Later, I call Paul. "Spare me," he says; dismissing my story as if I was telling him that he had pus on his burger. To pay him back for his attitude and really rock his boat I say, "By the way, our parents had sex, or are you too uptight to hear that."

He hangs up on me. We are all so good at shutting doors. Thank God Mac is so good at opening them.

"I'm missing you, Soph," he says huskily when I call him to say goodnight.

"Me too, you," is all I can manage since I'm nearly falling asleep.

"Need you next to me, babe," he says, our shorthand for wanting to make love. The idea trickles over me, puts a smile on my face and I tingle.

"I just love you," I whisper, feeling his strength, needing him perhaps more than he needs me.

"Just wait till I get my hands on you," he closes with and I make some semblance of a sexy purr before whispering goodnight.

FORTY-FIVE

We have run up against a new problem. Peekay! It was my misconception that we could leave Peekay with Nelly while we headed south. Unfortunately for us, Nelly has the opportunity for a ride to visit her daughter in Ohio during the time we go to Louisville and she's asked if we'd mind making other plans for Peekay. Hey, if I were Nelly I'd go just for the excuse to get out of having Peekay in my house. No one else really wants a big fat lazy cat that will shit on the floor and rip your furniture to shreds. Mom refuses to consider a kennel, big tears well in her eyes at the mention of it. She looks so sad that I can hardly bear to look at her, so Peekay wins this round, but I'm not sure how he's going to like being in a cage all day.

***

Other than the Peekay problem, things are coming together. I've contacted various health care agencies and gotten many referrals for live-in caregivers. Maybe Izzy and Paul will find time to sort through the information and put things in place for Mom's return home. I certainly can't leave her alone when we get back.

Paul's secretary calls to set a "con call".

"Sophia, if I could break away from this trial I would come to the rescue of the cat," he begins. "However, since that doesn't seem likely, how about a white lie? Why not tell Mom that I'm going to take care of the cat, then stick the cat in the kennel. She'll never know the differences if she's as bad as you say."

"This isn't really about the cat, it's about Mom," Izzy says. "Mahatma says that Peekay is a metaphor for what we are trying not to face. Mom doesn't want Peekay to go to a kennel because he could be mistreated. It's the same about Mom, isn't it?"

"What?" Paul shouts.

"I have been praying on this and I'm just starting to get in touch with my feelings. I just don't want to ever put Mom in a nursing home where she could be abused or even molested."

"Jesus, Izzy, you hit the nail on the head. I can't imagine Mom in a nursing home." Paul sounds like they've just made a great discovery.

"Me neither," I add.

"One time I had to have a will signed by one of my clients who had just moved into a home. The pee smell made me gag when I was in the lobby. My poor client was dirty and his eyes told me stories I didn't want to hear."

"Thanks for sharing," I grunt.

"Hang on, Sophia. Everything I read tells me that to take her into one of our homes would eventually become too great a burden. We'll have to convene on this."

"Mmm," is all Izzy can manage.

***

The guilt's are upon me. By process of elimination I know that Paul is hoping I'll offer to take her back to Canada until she needs hospitalization. Izzy is in no shape and Paul's marriage would never survive. But I can't do it. In the little time I've been with her I've found myself being short with her, and if it were a long term situation, I don't think I could do it. What I really mean is that I don't want to do it. Does that make me a horrible daughter? Am I that selfish? This whole thing sucks.

FORTY-SIX

I promise Mom we can make a nice leg of lamb for dinner. "Yummy," she says and gets busy setting the dining room table. I stop what I'm doing to watch her in action. Expertly, she whishes out the white linen tablecloth, centering it on her first try; next, the china and crystal. She dances around the table lost in some kind of time warp until she's finished.

"Polish the silver now dear," she says sounding remarkably like the woman who made the best dinner parties in Barcelona. What the hell, I say to myself. Why not?

Then I notice what she's done. The table is set for eight even though it's just the two of us.

"Expecting company?" I stupidly ask.

No answer. The quizzical look comes instead.

"Mom, there are just two of us."

"Nonsense, girl. She points to each place setting." Daddy at the head, Mummy at the tail, me next to Daddy, Frederick with me, Theo sits next to Mummy."

Well, not quite, but remarkably she hasn't stumbled over one word and. Instead, she looks at me like I'm nuts so I wonder who she thinks I am.

"Magdalena, go to the bookie to pick up the meat."

Okay. Magdalena was our cook in Barcelona, a short, squat Basque with a long black braid down her back. She might have been four feet, eight inches tall. My grandparents never visited us in Barcelona so that dot doesn't connect either.

Oh this poor woman! How can I take her to Louisville to make a presentation? She doesn't remember most of her life, it would seem. I see disaster looming like a dark cloud.

"Ready to go grocery shopping, Mom?" I ask, not even beginning to imagine her response.

"Sure, dear. I'll just get my cat." Wham-o. Maybe I'm the patient.

***

We pull up to Jerome's Grocery and I remark how some things never change. The same green and yellow awning shades the big windows in the front of the store; the old shopping carts are a little rusty but in the same place as when I was a kid. I take a deep breath, feeling safe.

Dummy.

If you want some really sick entertainment take an Alzheimer's patient to the grocery store. She keeps herself very busy taking cans off the shelves and putting them back in different places. Then she hollers that everything costs too much money and the grocer is a thief. I was so embarrassed for her but she was laughing her head off.

Somehow we made it out of there despite the fact that she kept taking my money from my hand and offering only half to the cashier. With winks and whispers, promises to come back and settle up tomorrow, I get her out the door and in the car. I am laughing and crying as I drive home, imagining the worst in Louisville, ignoring her shrieks over imaginary roadblocks, gangsters chasing us, and threats that my father will be furious if we don't refill the gas tank.

FORTY-SEVEN

The lamb is delicious. I put a big dollop of mint jelly on my plate and run each slice through the sweet sauce. Mom does the same. In fact, she is mimicking every thing I do. I take a bite; she takes a bite. I put my fork down, so does she. I'm feeling the meanies coming on but as Edith Bunker would say, I stifle myself.

After dinner, I decide not to water down her bourbon so I can get a good night's sleep. Then she surprises me with one of the most lucid conversations we've had since she arrived in Canada. As a bonus, I've finally crack the code on why Peekay has this name. As we are having our toddies (diet coke for me), Mom gets on the subject of South Africa, probably because Nelson Mandela was on the news five minutes ago. Anyway, Mom launches into a choppy, but rather coherent monologue against apartheid and Adolph Hitler.

"White people worse than blacks," she pronounces. "Look at Africa." I'm sucked in immediately grabbing onto a ray of hope like a drowning sailor. Mom jumps up from her chair and stands in front of me. "Read *The Power of One*," she says, then slams her fist into my shoulder, yelling, "One person *can* make a difference!"

According to Mom, a little boy named Peekay was the hero in this story. "The kids called him Piss…. Peekay stands for Pisskopf—piss head." Mom stomps her foot, then closes her eyes, clearly exhausted by the effort. Peekay is a very appropriate name for a cat that can spray with such force you can hear the splash from ten feet away.

So there, a family mystery has been solved. And I, for one, love the story.

A few minutes later, she tears the bookcase apart looking for the book, which she passes over several times. Her reading is a terrible concern. So are these bursts of anger.

***

To get things moving for our getaway in the morning, I decide to pack up the car. Mom checks each piece of luggage that I carry out and discuss what's in it and why we're taking it. "Where are we going *this* time? Can't we stay home?" she asks. "I don't want to get in the car again." Can't say I'm too happy about the idea myself.

"We're going to the Kentucky Derby, Mom. We need to drive the car there."

"Oh, that's nice." She offers a big smile, even a little hug. "Do you have the book?" God, she remembers!

"Right there," I say, pointing to a box I have placed in the trunk. And just to put to rest any loose thoughts I may have as to the wisdom of this trip, every once in a while Mom stops me and asks, "Are we really going to the Derby?" When I answer, "Yes," she rubs her hands together gleefully like a little girl and smiles. Tomorrow we will head out just as soon as I can get Mom up and on the road.

FORTY-EIGHT

W*e now have a huge problem*! I'm so upset with my brother and sister that I can't talk to anyone right now. Instead, I leave an urgent message with Paul's secretary to tell him to check his email and to call Izzy and tell her to do the same. I'm ready to pack my bags and have Mac come to get me. They need to step in, either one of them, or both. I don't give a shit.

To:	PVorelli@lawfrm.com
	IsabelaCam-aok@hotmail.com
From:	Sophia@peisland.net
Subject:	**READ THIS OR DIE**

1   Paul—I think it stinks that you would even suggest that Mac be the knight in shining armor. Mac is highly allergic to cats and to be blunt, we'd have to kill Peekay, have the house professionally fumigated, etc. But then you KNOW this. Although I don't doubt that you are in the middle of a big trial, it seems all too convenient that you are never ever available to help out, except to send checks, not that they aren't appreciated.

2   Izzy—the fact that you laughed when I called from the emergency room to tell you that I

broke my foot makes me want to strangle you. I did not think your "footloose" or "hot foot" remarks were funny. It must be wonderful to live in Marina Del Rey, smoke pot, which I believe is very expensive, and plead poverty to me. Or better yet, tell me your job is in jeopardy. Since when did that ever stop you?

3   Both of you: put your heads together and work this out. My RIGHT foot is broken— I can't use a gas pedal and Nelly is nearly blind and shouldn't be driving to the grocery store. I'm sorry to inconvenience you but I can assure you that when that fat shit Peekay tripped me and I fell down the porch stairs landing with my skirt up around my ass just as Duane St. George drove up, I lost my sense of humor. It's bad enough to see my 7th grade boyfriend looking trim and gorgeous as ever, but it totally ruined me to see him gazing at my prim cotton panties, instead of black lace lingerie.

I quit. I mean it.
Sophia

I leave my laptop on waiting for a reply. The phone rings twice but I refuse to answer it. It's not Mac; I've already called him.

To: Sophia@peisland.net

        IsabelaCam-aok@hotmail.com

From: PVorelli@lawfrm.com

Subject: Sorry, sis

Dearest Sophia,

How is old Duane, anyway? Just kidding. Listen, we'll work this out. In the meantime, don't take it out on Mom. It isn't her fault and if I hear the cat is dead, I'll know you poisoned him. Hang in there. Izzy and I are caucusing. We are going to call you in few minutes. Please pick up the phone.

Love,

P

A few minutes later, both lunatics call.

"Help is on the way!" Paul says, pausing to sip his Starbucks double latte mochacheeka, whatever the Hell that is. "Fiona is coming to the rescue. She's on her way to the airport right now! She'll be there by morning, so don't worry about a thing. She's a good driver, loves her grandma and Izzy and I think it's a great solution!"

I'm quiet for a moment and then I erupt.

"Fiona!!! Now that's what I call rocket science, clearly, you idiots have lost your minds. Think about what could happen. She's a junkie and I'm a drunk! Forget it. Of all the idiotic ideas, this one takes the cake. Fiona may be my niece and I love her, but she is fresh out of rehab and we all know about relapse. I would have to hide my pain pills, for God's sake, to say nothing of my wallet. I'm sure this is all your idea, Izzy.

Yeah, live vicariously through your kid. Let her do your job, Izzy. Hear me, *your* job."

"Okay Soph, you didn't disappoint us with your response," Paul the Prick says.

Izzy can be heard chanting as he speaks. Now, in a voice reminiscent of someone who is channeling Mother Teresa she says, "My daughter needs to be greeted with love and kindness and not your pompous, self-righteous bullshit."

Well, so much for the sainted lady.

"She's suffered and paid dearly, Sophia. So watch your mouth and cut her some slack. She loves you and would be crushed if she knew what you are saying."

It's my turn." Too bad you didn't feel so protective of your daughter while she was growing up. I suppose if she relapses, it will be my fault. Then again, we could both relapse and I could kill myself."

"Shhh, shhh," one of them is trying to shush me.

Ah, yes, it's Paul. He launches into two minutes of how sorry he is, it must hurt like hell, he wishes he could come and yada yada and then he starts to defend their suggestion.

"Fiona has been through hell—two years in rehab and sober houses—and she's fantastic. I think that you're in no position to judge her capabilities or her sobriety since you never made it down to Florida to visit her, like we did." Rub it in, Paul; obviously you don't know how much it costs to fly to Florida from PEI, especially since Canadian dollars are like funny money in America. Anyway, Paul's on a tear.

"Fiona may have been a junkie, but she isn't anymore and she's proud of her courage. The fact that our niece is willing to drive her aunt and her grandmother to Kentucky under less than ideal circumstances speaks volumes. She wants to give back to all of us for what she put us through, Soph, so relax and go with the flow. Can't you hear Izzy crying on the other line?"

"Crocodile tears," I hiss.

"Hey girl, it wasn't so many years ago that we were rolling j's. And I recall a hash brownie recipe you were famous for. It'll be okay, Soph, we know you're under tremendous pressure and we're eternally grateful. She'll be there by two."

Click.

Then Mac calls and I pick a fight with him. Duh.

FORTY-NINE

Fiona has arrived! I must admit that she looks healthy and wonderful in a flowing gypsy dress and big straw hat. The angles in her face are now softened by plump cheeks colored by a rosy glow. And no wonder. When she puts her packages down it's obvious that she's carrying more than a pie box. She's pregnant! My eyes signal her that I see her bump, but she pretends not to notice. Instead, she shrieks, "It's me, Gran, Fiona!"

"Lamb!" Mom shrieks back.

"I brought a lemon meringue pie, Gran."

"Goodie!"

"I'll put the kettle on." I grab my crutches and swing to the kitchen.

"A fine kettle of fish," I whisper to Mac who's busy at work.

"It just keeps getting more interesting, babe. Lighten up and go easy on her. She probably needs you as much as you need her."

***

Within ten minutes of her settling in, Fiona cuddles up next to Mom to sing "Come On-A My House" just like Izzy taught her when she was little. Mom joined in, forgetting most of the words, but remembering the tune.

It would've been nice to know in advance that Fiona was

bringing Cupcake, an aging English bulldog, but what the heck. This is going to be the trip from Hell anyway, what's another body in the car? It's nice to see that in spite of everything she's been through, Fiona is still the loveliest-looking blossom in the bunch of us Vorellis. Her boarding school manners are still there, and when she serves the pie she uses the good china and silver. I admit I'm watching to be sure she isn't stealing any of it like before. Actually, for the first time in weeks, I can take a little nap without one ear to the ground and worrying about Mom.

When I awaken, Fiona is brushing Mom's hair and putting makeup on her, but it all changes quickly when Mom asks for her baby.

"You don't have babies anymore, Gran. They're all grown up," Fiona explains.

Mom becomes agitated. "Bring me my baby now," she demands. Quick as a wink, Fiona dashes up to the attic, returns with one of her old dolls. She gives it to Mom, passing it to her carefully, as if it's alive.

"Support her head, Gran," she says playing along.

Mom takes the doll and presses its cheek to hers. "Ah," she sighs. With one deft move, Mom inserts her pinky finger into the doll's mouth, then rocks contentedly as the doll is "suckled". I choke up while Fiona pulls up a chair next to Mom and starts doing a crossword puzzle—something Mom taught her to do years ago. Fiona never looks up while Mom babbles baby talk to the doll, yet I'm sure I see a tear roll down her cheeks.

Later, I hear Fiona on the telephone with her sponsor. Clearly, this is difficult for her. I'm ashamed to admit it, but I hide my money. Fiona looks great, seems great, but she is an addict in recovery, and this is big-time stress, so I have to err on the side of caution.

"We can leave in the morning," she says when she returns from walking Cupcake. "Why don't you get some rest now, Auntie? I'm a light sleeper so I can listen for Gran."

I hobble to the bedroom and flop onto the bed, trying to ignore my throbbing foot. Fiona appears with a glass of milk, a plate of cookies and a look on her face that says she needs to talk. She puts the tray down and lies down next to me.

Fiona takes my hand and presses it to her belly.

"So, you're going to have a little bambino, honey. Does your mother know?"

After listening to her and sending her off to bed, I call Izzy.

"Your daughter is eight months pregnant and the baby's father has run off."

"No shit."

"Right. She lives hand to mouth and has no possible way of giving up her job for even a few months to care for an infant."

"What's she going to do?" Izzy quivers.

"I'm sad to say that she's going to give the child up for adoption."

There is a muffled sound and then Izzy screams, "Shut up, Mahatma! Sophia, keep this under your hat and don't tell Paul. I'll call you back."

"No, Iz, not until I'm finished. You need to find it in your heart to help your daughter. I told her she could live with us, but since she's a U.S. citizen she'll have to pay all medical expenses. Mac and I live on a pretty tight budget. Now I'm going to call Paul."

"Sophia, wait."

"Screw you."

"No, screw you. Mahatma and I will raise the child."

I hear a clang in the background which makes me laugh, until I get mad all over again. "Did you ever think that maybe you could help your daughter raise her child?"

"God, I'm such a selfish bitch, aren't I?"

"I don't know what you are, Izzy, I only know that we have to step up to the plate and do what's best for Fiona and the baby."

"Let me tell Paul, Sophia. I mean it."

"Go for it."

FIFTY

After an hour, my brother calls. He's laughing about something, doesn't bother to say hello, and just launches into his monologue.

"If it weren't so sad it would be downright funny. Here is our family tree. You there, Soph?"

"Yep.

"Maybe it's me, but this is getting even weirder. We have a drug addict who's pregnant, a new age lesbian grandmother-to-be who is meditating on all of this, and a future great-grandmother who is, shall we say, clueless."

"It's about as funny as an abortion," I chortle.

Paul babbles along, loving the sound of his voice. "Hey, look at me. I married the gorgeous and brilliant Alicia Banforth, but in a moment of drunken stupidity I knocked up our babysitter. Alicia, my sweet little women's libber, agreed to raise Malika along with our little Hillary. Like a fool, I agreed. Then to get even, Alicia had affairs with half the studs in town."

I haven't heard this last part before, now my curiosity is piqued.

"I believe she's seeing our optometrist at the moment. "

"Really," I say just to indicate I'm on the other line. He could care less.

"Hillary has returned the favor of having an illegitimate sister by earning three DUIs and flunking out of the University of Alabama, and that's pretty hard to do. That's my story."

"Well, it's America, what can I say?"

"Don't say anything, stay focused. Let's do Izzy who did me the great favor of marrying Jay Bernstein, a really nice guy; my fraternity brother, as it was. She didn't bother to tell him that she was gay, or at least bisexual, so he ended up flipping out when he found her in bed with another woman. When he followed Izzy's lover out of their apartment, the woman tried to run him over in her Ford pickup. What was her name, Soph?"

"Jennifer," I answer, contemplating hanging up the phone.

"Right." So Jay pulled Jennifer out of the truck and sat on her while someone called the cops. When she rolled out from under little Jay, she beat the shit out of him, then took off before the cops arrived and Jay landed in jail."

"Paws, do we have to do this right now?" I scratch my head and realize I need a shampoo badly.

"Absolutely! Did my good man Jay learn his lesson? No way. He and Iz made up, made Fiona and pretended that they were in love. His family went batshit over the birth of their first grandchild and bought them a house so they'd be comfortable while Jay was in law school. So what does Izzy do, I mean God forbid she should be happy, settled, centered? She leaves him for Moonalisa Jenkins—God, I love that name—and forgot to come home for three months after Fiona's first birthday."

"You're being an asshole," I shout.

"Most assuredly. That's been my role with you for years, Sophia."

"You said it, I didn't."

"Okay, let me wrap this up for you. Jay got custody of Fiona who was raised by his mother until they put her in boarding school. Meanwhile, Moonalisa dumped Izzy for some chick attached to Jefferson Starship."

"Stop. You are reminding me that we are all crazy."

"This is fun! And now, after a long string of whatever, she's with a New Ager named Mahatma who can't even spell her name right. Meanwhile, I can never go to a frat reunion."

"Well, life sucks and then you die. Listen, Paw-Paw, I have to run."

"You can't run you have a cast on. Besides, now we're on to you, Sophia Mia, my darling sister who chose the hippie life with Mac up in PEI. She became a leader in island life, well respected, with lots of friends. Now this isn't half bad for someone like Sophia, except she could be doing so much more with her life."

"That's enough, bro."

"Well, at least you're happy and Mac is the salt of the earth. Don't worry, I won't mention Jack."

"You're really pushing me now." I tremble, debating if I should hang up on him.

"As for more about me, well it's like this. Mom is my buddy. She always has been and always will be."

I feel my heart twinge. As much as I wanted to hang up a moment ago, now I can't. Across the miles, I reach my hand to his State Street law office in Boston, clasp his fingers to my heart and together we bawl like babies.

"We've got to have another talk like this sometime," I manage to say.

"I know," Paul says and then I hear his childhood voice say "Later, alligator".

FIFTY-ONE

With a little trepidation, I call Mrs. Benoit in Louisville. The drawl is thicker than expected, but absolutely charming; sugar will melt in her mouth.

"Darlin, ah cain't tell you ha happy ah am to heah yo voice," she says sounding just like Grand-Dahlia.

"Lou-ville is on pee-ins an' needuls jes waitin' to meet yo mama."

"Likewise, I'm sure," I answer politely. Oh brother, bring out the smelling salts. Hot damn if this isn't the dumbest thing we could ever do considering the shape Mom's in. I'm two beats from calling the whole thing off when she says, "the guvnah has arranged for yo' famlee to be in ah V-Ah-P box for the Derby. It's Kaintucky's way of thanking y'all."

Instead of demurring, I give up my chance to avoid bringing shame on our family. "Do you think we can get a third seat? My niece, Fiona, is joining us."

Mrs. Benoit hesitates. God knows the premium attached to these seats, but the gracious Southern magnolia assures me that this will be no problem. That's the good news.

The not-so-good news is that as part of the Derby celebration, they have planned a dinner in our honor the night before the Derby, and right before the Ball, to which we are also invited. *How will we ever pull this off?* I shudder at the thought of Mom at a formal dinner, with people, some fat, some dressed differently. I think she may have to be ill that night and I'll have to wing it. I'll figure something out. I never expected this!

FIFTY-TWO

We're Kentucky bound! Mom seems to be enjoying the trip, filling us in on all kinds of trivia.

"Rosemary Clooney is from Kentucky and she'll be at the Derby!"

"She died a few years ago, Mom."

"Liar."

"Maybe her nephew, George, will be there, Gran."

"Now *he's* what I call hot," my mother says.

And so it goes.

***

Mom's back to counting cows, pointing them out and making observations. It passes the time for her and I am now much more prepared for sudden shrieking without thinking that our lives are in danger. It still rattles Fiona, but she is a good driver so I think we'll make it.

Peekay, on the other hand, has found his voice, yowling constantly, worse than any Siamese I've ever met. God, he is an annoying creature. Mom, who also is having trouble listening to Peekay but for more sympathetic reasons than I, decides to take pity on him and lets him out of his cage while we are at the gas station. Of course, she neglects to mention that he is on the loose in the car.

Just as we enter the highway, Peekay jumps on the back of Fiona's seat, and flicks his tail across her cheek. "Damn" she shrieks as the car careens back and forth between lanes. Thankfully, there isn't another car in sight.

Mom thinks this is hilarious. Between peals of laughter, Mom manages to say, "Don't be a scarey cat!"

In the meantime, Peekay is scared to death by Fiona's reaction and scrambles around the car, fur up, bouncing off the windows, digging his wretched claws into whatever is in his path. Fiona has the car under control and back to a reasonable speed, but Peekay is still flying around.

After what seems like a very long time, Mom gathers herself enough for me to request between clenched teeth, would she be so kind as to "GETTHATGODDAMNEDCAT BACKINTO HIS CAGE!!!"

She glares at me. "Darlin, you too serious." That statement isn't exactly the tension breaker I'm searching for. Finally, Peekay slinks to the back seat and I'm able to grab him by the scruff of the neck. He fights frantically and I can't control him, so I throw him to Mom. She hugs him tightly and talks baby talk to him and they both start to purr to each other, which is fine with me. They both scowl at me from time to time as we drive the next few hundred miles in silence. Cupcake has not awakened during this encounter with Peekay, he just snores that godawful wheeze.

Paul calls later. "Ever hear of a cat harness?"

He's such a smartass. Not a bad idea though.

FIFTY-THREE

The morning is clear and bright. While Mom is dressing and Fiona leaves to put Cupcake and the caged Peekay in the car, I go to settle our bill. When I return, Mom is dressed, so to speak. The pants she wears come up to mid-calf. The blouse is mid-drift with the sleeves several inches too short. I stand in the door blinking, staring, while she applies her lipstick in front of the mirror.

Finally I clear my throat, "Mom, I think you have my clothes on." She looks in the mirror, and takes it in.

"Oh good, I thought everything shrank in the.... " she grabs for a word and misses. Then she goes over to the bed and sits down, looking fragile and lost.

A long silence.

"Don't know what's wrong with me," she says "So confused."

I sit next to her, taking her hand. "Mom, you're sick. You have a disease. It's called Alzheimer's."

"I'm fine," she says and then more quietly, "Just confused and afraid."

"I know, Mom."

"And then I get mad and...frus...."

"I know."

"I can't find anything."

"You're sick. And because you're sick you forget things. You can't help it." She nods, grasping at my explanation. "Your sickness affects your memory."

"Yes," she whispers.

I cup her face in my hands. "I'm here to help you, Mom. You aren't alone. Paul and Izzy and I will help you and Fiona is here right now." She looks straight into my eyes, knowing, and understanding. I hate this moment of her clarity. She looks at me with such trust, the trust of a child. "I know you will, Darlin," she says. I hold her tightly. My Higher Power is going to have to guide me through this.

While Mom is in my arms I realize how thin she is, shrinking into a stranger. I'm terrified she is going to die soon. Fiona blows her nose, turning away to hide her tears. Just as we're about to have a pity party, Peekay rubs against my cast and scratches his back. Mom thinks this is a riot; she laughs and laughs until she snatches him up and puts her nose to his. It is then that I realize Peekay is good for something else, besides comforting and being a friend to Mom. She feeds him all the tidbits she stores in her purse so I don't have to worry about her eating them herself after sitting several days in her purse. It's no wonder how he's so fat!

***

I've struck a compromise with Peekay; he spends part of the day in his carrier and part of the day loose in the car. Cupcake, on the other hand, suffers terribly from gas. Mom has been feeding him a bunch of Nutter Butters when we weren't looking and now he is farting his brains out. Still, the trip is going smoothly if you consider what could be happening. Most importantly, Mom is enjoying herself.

FIFTY-FOUR

A s we ride along, Mom takes out The Book. She thumbs through it page by page, mile by mile. Our Tennessee Williams moment is about to arrive.

"Mummy was a Southern belle. I curtsied before my ABCs." She bats her eyelashes and licks her lips.

"Did you tilt your head ever so pretty, Gran?" Fiona mocks my mother's drawl

"Pull over!" Mom demands.

"What's going on?" Fiona asks, looking in my direction.

"Don't worry, better do as she asks." I sigh, shake my head and wait to see what develops.

To our amazement, Mom treats us to perfect curtsies, her form impeccable, as a convoy of ten-wheelers whizzes by.

When she is back in the car she delights Fiona with descriptions of her boarding school—Miss Farnsworth's Finishing School for Young Ladies. I know that the school was in Boston, but Mom swears it was New York. "Albany," she says with finality so there's no point in arguing.

Later Mom announces "Mummy's family has colored slaves."

"Please call them African-Americans, Mom. No respectable person says "colored" anymore."

"Fool," she says shaking her finger at me. "Grand pappy was the first white baby in Louisville. His nanny is colored, my nanny is colored and Aunt Tillie Sue Ann is colored.

"Really?" Fiona and I chirp in unison.

"Yes, and never say nigra. That won't be said in our family."

"Aunt Tillie Sue Ann was black?" Now that I think back and remember her photographs, she was dark-skinned and handsome.

"No, she *colored*!"

Hmm.

FIFTY-FIVE

M om flips through the pages of the book, telling fragments of stories about each distant cousin, uncle, aunt or family friend. I have no way of knowing how accurate these stories are or if she knows who they really are. Probably they're a blend of many with some fantasy thrown in, but it doesn't matter. We love hearing her talk about "the good old days". She enjoys herself so much. This is such a contradiction to her reaction to the photos in the house just a little while ago!! This disease plays tricks with all of us. It takes her over an hour to tell this story, during which Fiona and I fill in the blanks and assist with words she can't remember. Still, we are enthralled with the family lore—truth or dare.

According to Mom, Lydia Lee Randolph was Melanie Greenfield's sister-in-law. After Melanie gave birth to a little 'colored' child, Lydia Lee took the child into her home and raised him. Simon Sheffield Randolph grew up thinking that his mammie and pappie had died of influenza. Simon was sent up north for his schooling, was smart as all get out and graduated from Yale. After Lydia Lee passed on, the family lost track of him. He changed his name to Sydney Foxe to become a stage actor, quite respected on Broadway. Of course he was stunning, with his coffee-colored skin, full, sensuous lips and the Greenfield's family high cheekbones and forehead.

It seems that Melanie, a very Gone With the Wind-ish name now that I think of it, never married and eventually moved to New York City where she lived off a family trust. She went to the theatre and saw Sydney on stage and fell head over heels in love with him. She pursued him with letters, even went so far as to wait at the stage door for him.

Now mind you, I am only imagining what happens next. Instead of rewarding our curiosity, she stumbles along, weaving tales about people I've never heard of. Finally, when we think we've got her back on track, she switches back to Rosemary Clooney and maybe she'll be at the Derby and that's it. We will never ever be told the end of the story. End of story.

"Maybe Gran's trying to tell us something," Fiona says.

"I think she's just trying to drive us crazy," I answer. Fiona clears her throat, checks the rearview mirror while I busy myself tending two of the grossest animals in the world.

"Mom, perhaps you don't know that Rosemary has passed away, dear. She was very sick and it was a blessing that she didn't suffer." I think it's best to break the news to her instead of having her running all around Louisville looking for Rosemary Clooney.

"Who?" she asks as if she's just entered the conversation.

"Rosemary Clooney," I answer patiently. She looks at me like I'm from Mars.

"Who?" I look to Fiona who's in the middle of blowing a giant bubble which she inhales too quickly and is now stuck on her face.

"You know, Gran, *Come-on- a-my-house...*" Fiona sings as she picks off sticky pink strands.

"Oh, I know that. Bing Crosby died ages ago." Mom frowns at both of us.

"You girls are stupid," she says, then blows a juicy raspberry at me.

I close my eyes. Maybe I can take a nap, wake up and have dreamed this whole month.

"Auntie Soph, there's got be some truth to some of this, somewhere. Call Uncle Paul and my mom to see what he knows."

"Look honey, I love you to death but I don't think we're black and you don't come from a musical family."

Fiona gives me a fierce look, begins to sing "Unforgettable" at the top of her lungs. The pitch is wrong, she's off key and downright horrible, just like Mom. Mom loves it so much that she keeps asking Fiona to sing it again and again until I slyly release Peekay from his cage to cause a diversion. Cupcake is more than happy to respond to the provocation by snorting at the errant cat who is rubbing his body against the dog's boney head.

***

Cupcake is the grossest dog I've ever seen. He eats, drools, wheezes, farts, shits, pisses, and sleeps. The only time he shows any emotion is when Fiona scratches him and he laps her with that huge tongue. He doesn't appear to have a neck, which might be why he can't breath right. He is so bow-legged he can barely get in the car, but wouldn't you know it, he makes it time after time. Mom drives me nuts as she imitates his wheezing...for hours.

Later, I tell Mac that Mom swears we have African American blood in our family.

"Works for me, baby" he says. "Black is beautiful."

On the other hand, Fiona wonders if the black gene will

pop out when her baby is born. "Actually, that would be very cool," she muses, and I agree.

Just as things settle down, Izzy calls for Fiona. After machine gunning her daughter with a burst of "motherly" questions Fiona grunts, "whatever" then hands me the phone.

"How's she feeling? Has she been to a doctor? Is she taking her vitamins?" Izzy sounds manic.

Fiona twirls her nose ring as I hold the phone out so she can hear.

"She is wonderful," I tell Izzy. "Not to worry. You've got some shit to work out. That's all."

I'll say.

FIFTY-SIX

The closer we get to Louisville, the more excited Mom becomes. With a child's wonder, she notices the change in landscape, the horses and the endless fences rolling over bluegrass slopes. She points and giggles, pleads with us to stop the car, and suddenly it's all worth it. Her joy is infectious.

"Horsies!" Fiona yells, pointing at some thoroughbreds grazing near a fence.

"Giddyup," I repeat five times before Mom reaches over the seat and yanks my hair.

"The horsies can't hear you," Mom says logically.

Being on this trip is like being in our own movie. If you think of the characters, our histories, our lives, I know we're just ordinary people, but that's the point. We're just ordinary people on a road trip—three generations laughing, crying, snipping at each other, and making up silently.

***

We pass acres of daffodils and jonquils, a yellow and white landscape that rolls along, bending and swaying, giving and taking, a powerful dose of springtime as we make our way to Kentucky. Fiona hums a tune for Mom, points to the sky as a threatening rain cloud passes overhead. Cupcake growls while Peekay's haunches rise.

CHARLOTTE JERACE

"Settle down," Fiona says softly and Cupcake drops his head, covering his ears with his paws. A clap of thunder precedes a torrential downpour. Fiona turns the wipers on; their monotonous metronome sets the beat for one of my favorite Elvis songs playing over the radio. After the first verse I join in. It isn't until I lie in bed that night that I realize how appropriate the lyrics are.

Seven lonely days
And a dozen towns ago
I reached out one night
And you were gone
Don't know why you'd run,
What you're running to or from
All I know is I want to bring you home
So I'm walking in the rain,
Thumbing for a ride
On this lonely Kentucky back road
I've loved you much too long
And my love's too strong
To let you go, never knowing
What went wrong
Kentucky rain keeps pouring down
And up ahead's another town
That I'll go walking thru
With the rain in my shoes,
Searchin for you
In the cold Kentucky rain,
In the cold Kentucky rain...
Kentucky Rain (words & music by Eddie Rabbit and
Dick Heard)

***

Fiona sings all the time and when she isn't singing she's talking about God. She is very spiritual for a member of this family, a result of her sobriety. She says, "God has chosen to keep me alive for a reason. Maybe it's to drive the car on this trip."

"I think it's a lot more," I answer.

She flicks back a loose strand of blond hair. "Hey, I don't question God anymore. God has the power to affect all of us. There are no coincidences. Everything happens for a reason." Mom reaches over and pats her hand so lovingly that it makes me ache. Fiona is her own person and I find myself forgiving her for the pain that she caused this family. Now if only God will tell her to take out the rings in her nose and eyebrow before meeting the ladies of Louisville.

FIFTY-SEVEN

When we make a pit stop, Fiona tends to Mom, giving me an opportunity to stretch my good leg. Standing back, I look at my beautiful niece and I can't imagine her sticking a needle in her arm. I can't fathom that she would do that to herself, or let anyone do it to her. When I asked her how she got the money to support her habit and she answered, "You don't want to know." I'm sure I don't.

In my nighttime prayers I say something special for Fiona. She's my flesh and blood. I just can't imagine her with a needle. It turns my stomach and makes my knees go weak.

The motion of the car often puts Mom to sleep. Now she's snoring right along with Cupcake. When Fiona smiles at me I realize that she has her mother's smile, slow, impish, dimply and innocent.

"You're the bomb," she says, with a wide grin.

"Yeah, sure," I say, going crazy from the cast, wishing I was, indeed, bombed.

"No, really," she insists. "I know that your leg hurts and the cast is driving you crazy, but you're still on this trip." Yes, by golly, I am.

"You're cute, you know."

Fiona chuckles and rubs her stomach. "Real cute with this belly. But seriously, you're so sweet to Cupcake, which is amazing because his gas is legendary."

I turn to look at Mom snuggled against the dog. Peekay is resting on the back of Mom's seat, one paw on Mom's shoulder, eyes closed, purring like a lawnmower.

"I know you didn't want me to come to the rescue, Auntie So."

I nod. "I feel like a jerk now, honey, but I won't lie, I had my reservations."

"You'd be stupid if you didn't. Hey, I'm a drug addict who's been in and out of the nut house and rehab. Plus, you're probably ashamed that I'm your relative and I totally understand why you'd feel that way." Her eyes are moist, but a trace of her smile remains. I get to thinking.

"Fi, I'm not ashamed of you, honey, I love you. I was concerned, that's all."

Fiona smiles, shakes her head and wags a finger at me. "You think I don't realize that you never leave your pocketbook near me?" Izzy's crooked grin is sweeter on her daughter's face.

I gulp, it's true. A part of me worries that she'll rip me off. The old Fiona would've cleaned us out, all the way to hell with a one-way ticket.

"Don't worry about it," her voice is strong and sweet. "I know that what I've done is always going to be part of my history. But today, this day, I am clean and sober, doing my Steps and reading from the Big Book every night."

***

Fiona sighs contentedly. I'm quiet, feeling we've said what we have to say. I watch a baby's foot roll inside her belly. She pats her stomach lovingly, a new expression on her face.

"What's going on in that gorgeous head of yours right now?"

"Watching Gran in Neverland. It's so weird. Gran does some things I've seen people do when they're partying. Although I don't remember most of my drug-hazed moments, I can remember some dudes on acid talking to horses and cows just like Gran does. I just pray she isn't on a bad trip."

"Or a bad drunk."

"I also pray that Gran knows how much I love her."

"She does, Fi, you can be sure of that."

We pass a pasture where beautiful horses are grazing but Mom is sleeping so soundly she misses seeing them.

"Does it bother you if I talk about...you know?"

"No, baby, you go ahead."

"One time when I overdosed, I woke up in the hospital and this Jamaican nurse was sitting by my bed. A cop was blocking the door, which is standard when they think you're trying to kill yourself. Anyway, the woman had this wonderful pure black face, the color of warm molasses. She was bending over me smiling, telling me I was going to be okay. I asked her why they didn't let me die and she said that I was too pretty to die."

"You didn't want to die, did you, Fiona?" Butterflies swarmed in my belly.

"Oh, I'm sure I didn't care if I lived or died, but Miss Madge, the nurse, did. 'Why would you want to go an' do a thing like dat?'" Fiona imitates the nurse's Island patois. "'Don' you have a special person in yo' family who loves you something strong an' would miss you so bad?'"

"I told Madge that no one loves a screw up, but she didn't listen. Instead, she asked if I had parents. I told her that my father was dead and my mom was crazier than I am. I just wanted the woman to leave me alone, but then I got a whiff of her perfume and she smelled like Gran."

"Shalimar," I said, knowing how it affects me when I catch of whiff of it.

Fiona nodded. "Madge had this warm, wonderful smile that covered the lower half of her face. God, she was gorgeous with these beautiful features and expressive eyes." Fiona smiles at the memory.

I'm impatient for her to continue. "So what happened?"

"Well, when I looked at her really hard I saw that underneath the smile in her eyes there was sadness and pity—the real emotions she felt for me.

She asked me who I knew that wore her perfume."

"Smart lady,"

"No shit. I didn't want to answer her because I was afraid I would feel something. So she waited for a minute and she asked, 'Was it your mumma?' I shook my head. You know that Dizzy is strictly natural scents, musk, cucumber, and rain. 'Ah, your gran-mumma?' Miss Madge stroked my hair so gently I could barely feel it. And that did it. I remember somehow managing to say 'yes' before I broke down."

My throat began to close as I imagined these images.

"So Miss Madge made a huge sigh and pulled me to her so she could rub my back. Then she asked me when the last time was that I called Gran to tell her that I love her."

"Did you call her?" If she had, Mom never mentioned it.

Fiona shook her head. "I could barely breathe I cried so hard just thinking about it, but when I stopped I was on the phone with Gran listening to her chat about her peonies and how she was watching the little ants crawling all over the closed buds, willing them to open. When we hung up I realized that I knew what peonies feel like with bugs crawling on them. All junkies know what it feels like to itch, that's why they always pick their skin. I used to stand in the mirror for hours picking my face, opening scabs, itching like crazy until my next fix."

My skin crawled hearing this. I know that Mac dropped acid a few times and we all did dexies, but no one would mess with heroin. We didn't know junkies, in fact, when Janis Joplin and Jimi Hendrix overdosed, we distanced ourselves from their music; I mean, if this is what a junkie sounded like it was kind of disgusting.

Fiona reads my silence.

"I wish I could tell you that the phone call with Gran was my turning point but that's fairy tale shit. The truth is that I got high within an hour of leaving the hospital that time."

"Fi, you don't need to tell me this, unless you want to, of course. Just promise me you'll change the subject if Mom wakes up."

As if on cue, Mom stirs, yawns, stretches and opens her eyes. Frankly, I was grateful. After all, my brother and sister aren't the only members of the family entitled to denial.

LOUISVILLE, KENTUCKY

FIFTY-EIGHT

It stopped raining the minute we got off at the Louisville exit. I thanked God for that because if Fiona sang *"Kentucky Rain"* one more time I might have jumped out of the car and sent her along with Mom. But that's all washed away now. We're here, the hotel is top of the line, and I have good feelings.

Our motley entourage gets a few strange looks in the lobby as we parade in. People probably think we're just some eccentrics here for the Derby. *Are they wrong?* The hotel manager is not thrilled when Mom points out that we're sneaking her cat in, not to mention Cupcake, but they take it in stride after learning that we are guests of Mrs. Benoit.

There's a note from Mrs. Benoit welcoming us to Louisville with a promise to meet in the morning at 10:00. This works out well, since I've made a hair appointment for Mom at 9:30. I can meet with Mrs. Benoit while she's under the dryer.

While Mom is in the bathroom, I share my concern with Fiona. "I still have no idea what to do about Mom's presentation. Maybe I should just tell Mrs. Benoit the truth."

"Which is?"

"That Mom is ill and can't make a presentation, here's the Book—see you at the Derby."

"You can't be serious. We can't rob her of her crowning moment. You can't do that, Aunt So. Forget it." Fiona attaches Cupcake's leash to his collar and heads for the door.

"His farts smell like a smell like rotten eggs—rancid ones at that," I bitch.

"I know, but he's my man and you just have to suffer if you want to sing the blues." She flashes that grin again and I relax.

After unpacking and freshening up and waiting for Mom to pee, we venture out. As we walk through the lobby Mom gathers herself into her full height, losing the shuffle that has begun to creep into her step. Now her strides are long and confident—Grand-Dahlia's daughter to the core. Her eyes take everything in as she slips into the role of one who is accustomed to such surroundings.

We are just bowled over by Louisville. Fiona and I have a real sense of history and a heavy sense of 'if only's'. Bluntly, if only our esteemed forebearer had held onto the family land after founding this wonderful city, we'd all be rich as Croesus.

"The old geezer could've spared a lot of us our current problems," Fiona says. I choose not to go down that road.

Everywhere there is talk of the Derby. There are street vendors hawking everything imaginable, mint juleps flow out of bars, parades seem non-stop, jugglers perform on every corner—it must be like Mardi Gras.

Being in a fancy hotel has a positive effect on Mom. She dresses for dinner without any help and lets Fiona do her hair and makeup. She's not even fussing about Peekay being in his carrier. A FedEx from Paul is slipped under our door. Five $50 bills are clipped to a picture of a man with his finger up his nose. Paul has neatly printed a caption that says, "Pick us a winner, girl!" I marvel at his thoughtfulness, with everything on his mind.

***

The dining room has a wonderful view of the city. The lights are dazzling, provide constant entertainment for Mom. I really don't think I could bear one of her comments regarding other diners, the décor, or other people tonight. I shouldn't have worried. The waiter seats her and comments on a few points of interest in the cityscape and Mom is enthralled. Mom even asks for a "doggie bag" for Peekay for her leftover trout. The waiter never bats an eye.

Fiona wolfs down a huge slab of beef and more veggies than I eat in a week! For dessert, we order Derby pie which is very sweet, but the whipped cream tower on top cuts it nicely. Fiona's been a love, tending to Mom so sweetly. God love her for rescuing us in our time of need, I say. If only the hardware could disappear from her beautiful face.

FIFTY-NINE

A t two in the morning the ringing of the phone awakens me. Someone asks if I might be missing an elderly lady and a dog, gives a description of Mom, and I nearly have a coronary. Her bed is empty. No need to panic, I'm told, they have her. She had left our room, roamed the halls, knocked on doors and awakened their guests. At least she is wearing my clothes! And Cupcake is with her. Fiona cries tears of relief, while I remain numb, trying not to give in to my feelings. Now, I seriously consider canceling the book presentation. This is a nightmare. If it wasn't so late, I would call my husband because God knows I need him.

The following morning, under Fiona's watchful eye, Mom is primped in the beauty salon leaving me free to meet with Mrs. Benoit, a patrician-looking woman who oozes genuine Southern gentility.

"Ah am so lookin' fo-wood to meetin' yo mutha," she drawls wonderfully.

"Well, I must tell you that we've been on a long road trip and my mother is quite exhausted and—I clear my throat—a bit confused by the trip."

Mrs. Benoit smiles sweetly, says nothing. "Of course, she is looking forward to this evening and meeting *you*, and she is so excited she is about attending the Derby." I smooth my slacks, pat down my silk knit sweater and return her smile.

Mrs. Benoit takes my hand, pats it ever so gently. "Ah unner-stan, Sophia. Truly ah do." Without missing a beat she's eager to announce that her parents had known Grand-Dahlia and Grandpa! "They were part of the same social set," she says matter-of-factly. Although she looks to be about Mom's age, I guess that by the time "the girls" would have been playing together our grandparents had moved on.

As I walk back to fetch the Vorelli beauties at the salon, I decide to just screw it and let the chips fall where they may. I love my mother and this is her dream—if she remembers it, so I'm going with the flow for the long run. Still, I can't believe how tense I am. Maybe it's from walking with the cast on, or just the stress that's been growing since Mom arrived on PEI. For whatever reason, my neck and shoulders feel like they're wrapped in steel bands.

***

Fiona is my salvation; she is teaching me how to meditate. "Picture a beautiful scene," she says softly. I close my eyes and think of the Island, our favorite beach, the sunset. "Breathe in and out slowly and stay in that wonderful place," she instructs. Later, as Mom naps, I realize that the knots in my neck seem a little softer. For a while I'm able to talk to my niece about my feelings and most importantly, my fears for Mom's future. Rehab taught her a lot, she's supportive—I need that.

SIXTY

Mac was my salvation after Jack died, even when I
didn't want him to be.

The accident happened at the end of our visit to
Jack's folks. We'd driven to the Appalachian Mountain Club
hut at Pinkham Notch the night before our big hike so we
could be on the trail at the crack of dawn. Seasoned hikers know
that in the White Mountains weather can move in fast and
furiously. In fact, the summit of Mount Washington is known
for having the worst weather in the United States. Rather than
stay with Jack's parents we decided to bunk in at Pinkham
Notch so we'd get up-to-the-minute weather predictions; only
fools would climb on Mt. Washington in iffy weather. We'd
gone to bed early that night. I'd shared a dormitory style room
with three other female hikers; Mac and Jack scored a double
in the men's section.

After stuffing ourselves with a huge breakfast the next
morning, we checked the weather information board one last
time. The temperature on the summit was only 36 degrees
that early in the morning, but the skies were clear and we
could expect good hiking weather for the next few days.

Our backpacks were stuffed with extra clothing, gorp—a
mixture of nuts, raisins and M & M's—a hard salami, and
water. We'd planned to spend the night at Lakes of the Clouds
Appalachian Mountain Club hut, and then climb to the

summit the next morning before hiking down on the Lions Head Trail.

Jack had been ravenously hungry that morning. He was still stuffing apple cider donuts into his mouth as we headed up the trail. When we reached the little ranger's cabin at Hermit Lake, Jack drank a whole container of apple cider as we took in the view. "Drink lots of water right now," Jack had instructed, as we sat on rocks, resting before tackling the headwall. Mac was quiet as he studied the topography map. He suggested that Jack take the lead, with me in the middle. I remember thinking how lucky I was to be out in that spectacular setting with my two favorite guys, while worrying that I wouldn't be able to make the climb. The Tuckerman's Ravine trail is very steep, climbing over 600 feet before the horizontal crossover.

Even though the trail was rated difficult, it was packed with hikers. Many of the younger hikers wore shirts bearing the name of their prep schools. I remember an Andover sweatshirt and a Choate T-shirt, and the red-flannel shirt Jack had tied around his waist. Then there was a mountain man with a beard that reached half-way down his chest. He had a frisky dog with him that wore a purple bandana. It's crazy the things I remember.

I had done pretty well keeping up with Jack and Mac as we struggled up the trail. Because it was so crowded, we took only short breaks to catch our breath and take in the awesome scenery. Touches of autumn color stretched for miles as we looked across the tree tops that fringed the ravine. It was truly mind-blowing, as Jack had promised. As we neared the crossover trail, Jack turned to look at me. Rivers of sweat dripped from his face. "Dat's my girl," he'd said, proud that I had kept up with him. When he turned to continue I heard him curse in French under his breath. A large black dog was bounding across the top of the ravine and scampering towards us. We had to press our bodies into the mountain to let the dog get by. With bulky backpacks strapped on our backs, this was tricky at best.

Finally, we reached the top of the ravine. All we had to do was cross over the narrow footpath and it would be easy climbing the rest of the way. When we were half way across Jack noticed someone waving his arms in our direction.

"Hey, you asshole," he yelled at Paul. Jack turned to me and said, "Your nutty brother's here." I turned and told Mac who'd laughed and said, "You've got competition, Sophia. Your brother thinks Jack is a god." I saw Paul and waved.

Then it happened. "Watch out," Mac had yelled. I turned to him in time to see a flash of black. I felt something rub my leg, then Mac's eyes registered shock as his mouth opened and he tried to scream. When I turned back to Jack, he wasn't there. I heard an ungodly shriek and there was my Jack spiraling down the six hundred foot drop to the jagged rocks at the bottom. As I leaned over to see Jack land, the weight in my backpack shifted and I nearly went over, as well. Mac grabbed me just in time.

I don't remember how we reached the bottom of the ravine but Mac said that he practically carried me part of the way. Paul had caught up to us and was crying and praying to God, while calling down to Jack to hang on. When we finally reached Jack, Paul cradled his head and began to yell at him. Mac held me back, shielding my eyes, as he made the most frightening sobbing sounds. Without looking at Jack, I knew that he was dead. Mac and Paul were wailing and I finally freed myself so I could run to Jack. His head was lolled over to the side and it didn't take a doctor to know that he'd broken his neck. His eyes were wide open and unblinking and when I went to kiss him I saw that his skull had been cracked open. It was at that moment that I lost my mind.

***

I have no recollection of the weeks that followed Jack's accident. I know from Mac that my family arrived and took me home to Wisconsin.

Although I returned to Ann Arbor to start my senior year, I dropped out after a few days, stayed in the apartment and began drinking hard. But don't be fooled, I drank hard *before* the accident, so I don't blame my alcoholism on it. The difference was that finally I had an excuse to be drunk much of the time. Mac had tried to take care of me but he, too, needed consoling and I had nothing to give. Instead, I returned to Wisconsin to our cottage on the lake. There, I drowned my sorrow until finally, out of booze and out of money, J-stroked to the middle of the lake, yelled Tippy-canoe-and-Tyler-too, and, praying for the eternal nap, I capsized Grand-Dahlia's birch bark treasure.

SIXTY-ONE

Mom awakens from her nap refreshed. Our outfits, just returned by the concierge, are hanging where Mom can see them. When she spies her dress she says, "What a lovely dress," and after a small pause, "I have one like it."

"This *is* your dress, Mom" I say, offering her a smile and calling on my patience.

"Goodie," she says. "Let's play dress up!"

I start to make small statements about going to dinner and presenting the book tonight, unsure how much to say or how much would register. In the meantime I head her off in the direction of the bathroom.

The hotel has heated towel racks, bubble bath and all the other shower/bath paraphernalia that luxury hotels are so good at providing. Mom is intrigued with all the little bottles and taking her into the tub is a pleasant enough task. She soaks for quite a long time as Fiona sits on the toilet seat reading, letting her enjoy this time.

While she bathes, I call Mac. "What would happen if we get up there and she refuses to give Mrs. Benoit the book?"

"You're being a worry-wart, Soph."

"Or, what if she makes one of her loud and rude comments about someone at our table or anyone for that matter? One inappropriate comment and we could be out on our ear, no matter what our good intentions are"

"Well, Fiona could go into labor." He thinks he's being funny, but I tuck the suggestion away.

"Just tell me we'll get through it, Mac."

"God is good, babe. Wish I was there."

"Me, too."

***

After Mom steps into her dress we help her put on her diamond earrings and her diamond and sapphire bracelet. She steps back from the mirror to assess herself, pleased by what she sees. She looks beautiful and elegant. I finish dressing and put Peekay back in his cage, deftly avoiding the swipe of his claws.

And then there's Fiona! Izzy's attempts to raise a laid-back surfer chick daughter have failed! If she could see her tonight her socks would roll up and down. Fiona opens the bathroom door where she's been holed up for a long time and my jaw drops. The girl in the baggy sweater, gypsy skirt and Birkenstocks has disappeared and out comes Fiona, looking more like a debutante than debutantes look these days. All hardware has been removed from her nose and eyebrow and that glorious hank of blonde hair is knotted up in a French twist. She looks breathtaking in a long black silk tunic over slim black silk pants, which almost hides her pregnancy. Mom loans her a pair of pearl earrings and I have great pleasure fastening Grand-Dahlia's pearls around her throat. What a stunner!

SIXTY-TWO

We're finally ready. Mom sits down and checks her watch. "Time for a toddy." Great! The last thing I want her to do is have a drink before we even get there. I know there will be plenty of Mint Juleps being served tonight, that's been one of my many worries during the day. I tell her to wait for famous Mint Juleps and her interest is piqued.

When I gather up The Book, I flip through the pages one last time and a recipe for Mint Juleps falls out. I make a mental note to give it to Paul. Then, I check Mom and myself over one more time, get the few notes I'd written during naptime and head for the door. Mom stops and sits down again.

"What is it?" I ask. Silence. "Mom?"

"You two go on, dear." She flicks her boney fingers, shooing us.

"No, you need to come with us," I say, trying to figure out what the problem is, if there is a problem. Fiona's hand is outstretched to Mom, but it's a Mexican standoff.

We are quiet for a minute until she says, "Go without me, dears." As tempting as this offer is, I know we can't leave her alone and deep down feel it is important for her to come tonight. After all, this is why we're here. All the ups, the downs, embarrassments, aggravations, tender moments and laughs—all of which I know I will learn to treasure, have been just as important as tonight. But, tonight's the night! I don't understand the present hesitation, but I'm willing to wait it out.

I don't want to argue or upset her so I sit down with a magazine as Fiona busies herself straightening the room, calling the desk for tomorrow's wake up call and chatting away. It's very tender watching her cleanse the folds of her pathetically wrinkled bulldog and I can't help but think what a great mother she would be.

I had already planned on a late departure to cut down on cocktail hour, but now it's time to go, fashionably late is one thing, but being the guest of honor and very late, is another.

"Ready to head downstairs, Mom?"

No answer.

"Mom?"

She crosses her legs, straightens her skirt, and with the look of a teenager waiting for her first date says, "I'm waiting for your father to pick me up."

"What?"

"I'm waiting for your father."

"What?"

"He's picking me up."

Fiona stifles a sob.

I take another deep breath; blink a lot while my mind races and then I realize that she is waiting to complete her ritual. All her preparations had always been for Papa as much as for herself. All the pampering was just that, pampering and nice, but the overall goal was for her to please Papa and watch the delight she could bring to him by simply making an "entrance" and walking proudly together, arm in arm. Now, her preparations complete, she is waiting for him. I can only imagine the triggers that are firing in her brain as she is all dolled up. I remember how she would check herself over and over for the love of her husband. She was so seductive; she'd reach for her throat, stroking it softly, and then lock eyes with my father. I realize now how hot it was between them. She'd call him "Daddy" and slide up on his lap. He would tickle her and she'd squeal and cover his face with kisses, purring like a cat. God, how she loved him! Maybe one of the benefits of her disease is that she thinks he's still alive. She's forgotten how he died on the operating table after his appendix burst in Malaga.

Having finally figured out what the issues are, I have a plan. I grab the phone. When Mom comes out of the bathroom, I dial the operator and whisper for her to ring our room. She rings right back and I say in a nice clear voice, "Okay, Papa, I'll tell Mom that you'll meet her there."

Mom looks and me, then smiles widely.

"That was Papa. He said he was running late and he would meet you there."

"What?" I repeat 'the message'".

Mom reaches for her purse, "Let's go."

I wonder what will happen when we get there and Papa isn't there, but for now, Fiona and I gather up our things and hurry to follow Mom. We meet at the door, smiling as conspirators.

SIXTY-THREE

Thankfully, I don't have to worry too long about how the outcome of my little performance will play out. As we enter the private dining room, the festive mood of the Derby, the Historical Society's displays, and the grand decor for the occasion takes my mind off my troubles momentarily. Nor do I have to worry about Mom looking for Papa. She is as engrossed as I am, taking in all that is around us. Immediately, we are delivered Mint Juleps, which I graciously take, then set aside. Fiona comes out of nowhere and hands me a Perrier. Such a trooper, that girl.

Mrs. Benoit quickly spots us. "Toodle-loo, Loo-wah-ville loves ya" she chirps. She's a vision in flowing orange sherbet silk with wafts of Hermes 24 Fauborg surrounding her. Following introductions, she asks, "What'd y'all think of Kentucky after your first day?"

Mom sighs, "Bluegrass! The horses! Ooo-la-la."

Mrs. Benoit goes on about their families, then ushers Mom over to a display of photographs where she points out a photo of both their parents together.

"Can I have that?" Mom asks, reaching for the photograph.

"Course you can," Mrs. Benoit says. Ah have mo-ah."

Mrs. Benoit continues to point out different people and places. Mom is pretty quiet; I have no idea if she is taking it in, but acts the perfect listener with appropriate ohs and ahs. In what I think is the knick of time, we are called to dinner.

***

There are round tables of eight and to my great relief I'm able to seat Mom so that she faces a large screen which continually runs clips of tomorrow's Derby lineup. The horses are shown galloping through the fields, being groomed, and racing.

Mom is seated between two dashing Southern gentlemen. A Clark Gable look-alike takes it upon himself to narrate the clips for Mom, who seems to have no trouble falling into the role of southern belle, as she remembers it. She enjoys having this man entertain her, hanging on his every word, batting her eyelashes, holding herself erect, and gently patting his arm. She enchants him, even when she flicks out her tongue, almost sticking it out, but then drawing it back in to instead bite on her lower lip, giving him a provocative look.

Fiona and I begin to relax until the man on Mom's left says, "Why, Sugah, you haven't touched that Mint Julep of yours. Don't you like it?"

It's true that she's hardly touched it. As she screws up her face in disgust, I tense for her insult and can't think quickly enough to ward it off.

She sticks out her tongue, "Eck." A beat seems to go on forever as she sits there so primly, the tip of her tongue reaching the dimple in her chin. I will her to pull it in.

No one says anything for a second or two until the gentleman suggests, "Too sweet, in'nt it?"

Mom turns her head just like Grand-Dahlia used to, winks and says, "I'd prefer bourbon. Forget the rocks."

The man slaps his hand down on the table. "That's my girl," he laughs. Then he orders two fresh drinks, one for her and one for himself. I swig my mineral water while Fiona blows bubbles in her diet Coke.

We muddle through dinner. Mom nibbles at her meal, preferring to watch the images flashing on the screen behind the head table. Fiona is also quiet, taking it all in. Every so often, Mom points at an image that she finds interesting, but says nothing, leaving us to wonder, which is okay by me.

Between dessert and coffee, while many people are up to stretch and digest, I take Mom's hand. "We'll be presenting the book to Mrs. Benoit soon and we'll have to go to the front of the room." She has that vacant look, says nothing.

Once our coffee is served, Mrs. Benoit walks up to the podium and quiets the crowd. Allright, God, the moment has come. I barely breathe, pray silently, while offering a frozen smile.

Fiona is introduced first.

"Ah have the pleazuh of introducin' the youngest Campbell heah, Miz Fiona Campbell Vorelli Bernstein."

I secretly smile as I'm sure some of the bluebloods in the audience recognize the Jewish name and most likely shudder.

My beautiful niece stands, nods elegantly, offers a noble wave, then and then turns to me.

"Next, puh-lease give a Lou-aville welcome to Miz Sophia Campbell Vorelli MacDougal who drove her momma heah all the way from Canada."

I stand up, knees shaking and manage to warm my smile. There is polite applause.

"An fah-nally, the belle of the ball, hailin' from the great state of Kain-tucky, Miz Agatha Rose Campbell Vorelli, thuh great, great, gran'chile of Mistah Daniel Duke Campbell, our foundah."

Mom floats from her chair as the crowd cheers wildly. She tilts her head to the side, lowers her eyes, and blows them a kiss. She holds everyone in the room in the palm of her hand by the time we arrive at the podium.

Mom stands between Mrs. Benoit and myself as I read my short spiel giving some background and speak briefly how pleased the family, especially my mother, is to have this book back home where it belongs.

"Amen," Mom says, getting a chuckle from the audience.

Now the reason for driving over a thousand miles, to fulfill my mother's age-old dream is upon us. Fiona has her fingers crossed behind her back and I've ripped off another silent prayer. It has come to this moment.

I smile at my mother. "Mom, would you please give Mrs. Benoit the book." By then the applause has grown louder. And Mom is clutching the book to her bosom. She looks down, runs a hand over the leather cover, and then simply passes it to Mrs. Benoit. She is about to take it in her hands when Mom pulls it back.

I'm about to have a coronary.

Fiona slides forward and whispers something in Mom's ear. Mom smiles at her, then plants a big juicy kiss on the cover of the book. She then hands it proudly to me! In a stupor, I, too, follow my mother's example and quickly kiss the book before passing it to Fiona, who also kisses it before giving it to Mrs. Benoit. Just like that, simple as Derby pie. The Book has passed through three generations of Campbell women in front of the Louisville Historical Society and the crowd erupts. Above the din, Mrs. Benoit leans into the microphone, beaming at the book. "Thank you evuh so much."

Mom stands vacant-eyed but just when I prepare to say something in return Mom pipes up, "Take care of it." She smiles graciously, dips her head to the audience, who continue to applaud. Fiona and I beam through our tears as the room breaks into "My Old Kentucky Home".

As we walk back to our seats, Mom looks resplendent, bathing in this attention. I can't be sure what she thinks or even if she is confused by tonight's events. All I know for sure is that she has played her part magnificently. For a brief, shining moment, I saw glimpses of the woman who presided over our family dinner table, wiping daintily at her mouth, teaching us manners, and scolding Paul. Why, dear God, have you let this happen to my mother? What kind of bargain must I make for you to reverse direction?

Before going to bed, I take the Mint Julep recipe to the front desk. They'll fax it to my brother.

Paul: you are the only one who can still take a drink and not need one every day for the rest of your life so for old time's sake here is Grand-Dahlia's prized recipe for Mint Juleps. It was tucked in THE BOOK. She was perfect! Love, Sophia

GRAND-DAHLIA'S MINT JULEPS
Make simple syrup this way:
Pour 1/2 cup boiling water over 1/2 c. granulated sugar; stir until sugar dissolves. Stir in 1/4 cup lightly packed fresh mint leaves. Cover and chill at least 4 hours. Strain. Store covered in the refrigerator. Then, pour the syrup into a tall glass, add 4 springs fresh

mint, crushed ice, 1/4 cup bourbon, 1/2 cup tonic water, and a little powdered sugar.

Too drained to talk, I text message Mac. "She did it."

SIXTY-FOUR

W e get our early morning wake-up call and I can't budge Mom. She is so exhausted from last night that I let her sleep since it's going to be another big day. Mrs. Benoit has arranged for us to have a little tour of a horse farm this morning, just to get in the mood for the afternoon.

It's a short drive out of the city to the farm. Mom is in heaven. She takes big breaths and says, "Smell the air!" You'd think she lived in the city. She is so cute. In a minute, she removes her shoes and runs across the grass, which is exceptionally green and soft after last evening's rain. Mom loves the smell of the grass. "Kentucky rain smells yummy." Most of all she adores the foals. She loves watching them canter around the paddocks, kicking up their heels and nuzzling up to the mares. It's a joy to see these beautiful animals in such magnificent surroundings.

***

We return to the hotel for lunch and a short nap. Fiona's belly seems to have popped since the morning, and I'm sure she needs some rest. Still, she convinces me that we should go out and enjoy the excitement. She's right. The streets are filled with magicians, clowns, music and gaiety. Mom loves it! We've festooned some ribbons on Cupcake and there's a new swagger in the old fleabag's footsteps. I promised Mrs. Benoit that we would come about an hour before post time to join her for a drink. The racetrack will be a busy place with lots of stimulation and a lot of noise. Mom will be too preoccupied with all the activity to get into too much mischief.

There are three messages from Izzy when we return. Finally, I have a moment to talk.

"Mom's so excited, Iz. This was a fantastic idea."

"God how I wish I was there. I remember so clearly how she used to get all dressed up on Derby Day and made us do the same."

"You were the cutest little kid," I smile to myself remembering how Mom would allow Izzy to wear one of her fancy dresses, yards too long, but what the heck.

"I felt like Miss America back then," Izzy says. "I can't stop thinking about her hats."

"Me, too, remember the one with the peach roses and pink peonies?"

"Gorgeous." It was. The flowers covered the crown and a grosgrain ribbon was tied in a bow with tails long enough to catch the spring breeze. Her hats were nothing short of fabulous and when Mom put one on she was Louisville society personified. Her blue blood flashed like a neon sign.

"I remember how you and Mom used to whip up a hat for you to wear."

Izzy laughs. The decoration of her Derby "chapeau" was a ritual that she loved almost as much as Christmas. She and Mom would sit on the glassed-in side porch that caught the Southern sun. There they would arrange fresh daisies and lilacs around the crown of one of her old gardening hats. Sometimes Mom would add pussy willows to give Izzy some height.

Room service delivers a huge pitcher of iced tea and *iced glasses*. A vase of fresh mint twigs is also on the tray. I sip while Izzy speaks.

"I was telling Mahatma how I had the pick of any of her costume jewelry, covering my neck, wrists and both ankles with dozens of beaded and enameled treasures. And how Mom and I would have a tea party where she taught me how to hold my cup."

"Pour, sweeten and stir," we say together, followed by chuckles.

The imminent Derby reminds me that Papa taught us all how to choose our horse and wage our bets. We kids wagered with our Monopoly money, while Mom and Papa really got into it. They'd put up the cash and then there were little folded pieces of paper, keeping secret between them which I later recognize as the promise of sexual favors. I know this because Papa said that no matter if he lost he would still win later that night.

Once the family was in full costume, Papa would take out the Hasselblad and snap our yearly photos. There would be a group shot, then a solo pose for each of us. For years, Mom kept a picture of Izzy in a Derby chapeau taped to the refrigerator.

CHURCHILL DOWNS

SIXTY-FIVE

As if this moment would ever come, we're off to the races absolutely resplendent in our Derby costumes. Mom looks divine in her blue suit and Fiona is radiant in a flowing hyacinth dress. I wear the yellow knit Chanel-style suit Mac treated me to just for this occasion, and we all have our Derby hats on. Mac and the kids will love the photos.

When we arrive at Churchill Downs, it's magical. I've never seen more nattily dressed people. Everyone looks sensational, polished and groomed, shiny and peppy in their carefully assembled outfits.

Walking into the Oval is wonderful; the faint smell of the horses mixes with the expensive cologne of their fans. We are wide-eyed, marveling at the most famous racetrack in America. My heart pounds when the horses and riders warm up on the track, magnificent in their silks. It's amazing to watch elegant animals with perfect bodies and glistening coats prance by, noble and arrogant, the best of the best. The Oval itself is immaculately landscaped, the track pristine, and the scent of the flowers overwhelming. Heated, pre-race debates are being argued everywhere while private bets are wagered. Everything is alive and vivid. Mom, Fiona and I are in awe.

We're ushered to our box where Mrs. Benoit and Digby, her reed-thin, gin-nosed husband, greet us warmly. Mrs. Benoit is a study in salmon silk, her hat, dress, shoes and purse all dyed to match. Fiona whispers "creamsicle" and I want to swat her.

Her salmon straw hat is decorated with a wreath of fresh lilacs which has given her reason to wear ropes of amethyst beads around her neck. A two-inch square amethyst ring weighs down her right hand. Despite it all, she can pull it off. She has the right accent, manners, affect—you name it. I find myself liking her more and more. Digby is already bombed, content to let his wife run the show. As we get comfortable, Mrs. Benoit introduces us to a few people whom we hadn't met last night. The gentleman who had been on Mom's left the previous night is there and when the tray of Mint Juleps arrives he's quick to order straight bourbon for Mom and himself. There was no need for us to have eaten lunch; trays of delectable treats are served.

After the first drink, Mom stares at Mrs. Benoit. She has that look she gets just before she delivers one of her remarks. I try to distract her, but her forehead is already crinkled so I prepare for the blow. Then she speaks, looking straight at Mrs. Benoit, both eyebrows arched. "That is the most...stunning outfit."

"Why, thank you, shugah!"

I can't believe my ears. Thank you, God.

The conversation turns to fashion although Mom is studying the horses going by. After glancing at her program, she declares "Picked me a winner. I need to bite."

"Bet", Fiona explains.

Yes, of course.

I remind Mom that I've placed her $5 betting money in her purse in hopes that she won't lose it before the race. When we get to the betting window Fiona gives her another $5 to place on the horse of her choice. When it's my turn I bet on Unearthly—a fitting name for our situation.

***

With half an hour to go before the big event, I shuffle over to a refreshment area to rest my leg up on a chair. It's fun gawking at the incredible outfits people are wearing. Then, above the din I hear Fiona calling "Gran, where are you?" A chill numbs my spine.

"I've lost her," Fiona cries. "I took her with me when I went to pee but she wouldn't come into the stall and promised to stand next to the door and when I opened it she was gone!" Fiona is hyperventilating and her cheeks are red as beets. We stare at each, our imaginations running wild, trying to decide what to do.

"I'm going to find a policeman," Fiona says. Before I can answer, she bolts off. Then, despite my bad leg, I run to the betting windows, praying that Mom is there.

There must be hundreds of people waiting to place a last minute bet. Finally, I see a flash of blue that is the same color as Mom's suit. Relieved, I bound towards it until the wearer turns around and it's not Mom. Now I'm scared; so scared that I imagine the worst and head back to my seat to wait for Fiona.

Lo and behold, Mom is there, sitting next to Fiona, waving a bouquet of flowers at me, flashing her toothy grin, and sticking out her tongue.

My heart beats in my throat as I slide in next to her, ready to scold her until she separates the bunch of flowers. With a flourish, she presents half to Fiona and half to me. "For you!" she says simply.

"So sweet," Fiona says.

I'm about to thank her, as well until upon closer look I realize that these flowers are artificial, some of them clearly very expensive.

"She was plucking away at some of the ladies' hats when the cops nabbed her," Fiona explains, stifling her laughter. I slide my bouquet under my seat, trying to hide the goods. Mom turns back to me just as I sit up. Spying the flowers, she reaches down and plomps the lilacs back in my lap.

***

The next thing I know, someone is kissing my cheek. I look up to see my baby brother grinning from ear to ear, stunning in a perfectly tailored tan linen suit, expensive looking shirt and Armani tie.

"Uncle Paul," Fiona exclaims. "Oh. My. God! How cool is this!"

Mom lights up like a Christmas tree!

"What a wondah-ful supp-rise" Mrs. Benoit drawls, offering her cheek to my brother. God knows when he hatched this scheme, but here he is, fawning all over Mom and Fiona, being so attentive to them, and then squeezing my hand. He's all piss and vinegar, our Paul.

In my heart I know that I love my brother, but why do I have such prickles going up my spine when I see him? Maybe it's because he's so smug and sure of himself. To the unknowing eye, one would think he has escorted us to the Derby. Never mind the trip, the worry, and my cast, no; here is Paul Vorelli, Esquire, dapper and suave. I love him and feel horrible for this little burst of jealousy, but, on the sunny side, he's taken charge of Mom, leaving me to relax and enjoy the race.

SIXTY-SIX

As the horses are lead to the starting gate, they practically glow. The lithe jockeys, glistening in their silks, focus on their steeds, tushies up, bodies coiled in anticipation. As they prepare for post position, we sing "My Old Kentucky Home" and it's a glorious moment. Even though I've heard it a hundred times, nothing sounds like a live performance. Fiona lets me know that Mom is singing "Take Me Out to the Ball Game" but no one can possibly hear her above the din.

As the horses reach post position, electricity is in the air, eyes are glued on the track. And they're off!

I can't stop watching Mom. The years and troubles seem to melt away. She doesn't care which horse wins, she just loves to watch them run. She's totally absorbed, yelling, "Come on, come on, run, boy, run." I know she's urging them all on, wishing them all the run of their lifetime. I can imagine Mom as a young girl, listening to the Derby with Grand-Dahlia, cheering her horse to the finish line. They used to bet pennies on the race and she was allowed sips of Gran's mint juleps. I can imagine that little girl, the excitement coloring her cheeks as she heard the announcer call the race. She was known to have an uncanny ability to pick the winner way back then. It's too bad that ability didn't return along with the other childish traits that I see today.

A beautiful dapple gray named Prince Karl's Passion

wins the race by a nose. He was a 50-1 long shot and paid handsomely. Of course, we didn't win, but it didn't matter. Everyone hugs anyway and congratulates the horses and jockeys on a good race.

When Mom stands, Fiona notices a big wet spot on the back of her skirt. She's had an accident. We devise a plan to shield her from embarrassment, Fiona behind her, Paul and I on each arm. We decline the after race party and go ahead with our plan to order room service, pack and be ready to head out in the morning.

Paul and I are going to have coffee together after I get Mom in settled. Maybe we can finally begin to sort out this mess.

SIXTY-SEVEN

The coffee shop is nearly deserted and that's not a bad thing considering the decibels that my brother and I reach. Unbelievably, Paul is still in denial. He's been drinking and it ticks me off that he's the only member of the family who isn't an alcoholic or a drug addict. Then again, I'd say his need to work 24/7 is just another kind of addiction.

"She's not as bad as you've described, Sophia and you really piss me off."

"You mean you'd rather she be drooling and vacant-eyed?"

He leans across the table, booms," Shut up!" and then settles back in his chair.

"You are the one in denial, sister mine..."

"Give me a break, my cast itches, I haven't had a good shower in a week and I don't want to sit here and be abused by you. Save that for Alicia."

My blow startles him, an angry glint burns in his eyes. "And you're the perfect wife to the long-suffering, Mac, right?"

Bullseye, goose bumps rise on my arms. Paul shakes his head so arrogantly that I have an urge to slap him.

"When Alicia and I first met I told her that you the kind of kid that never got dirty when you played outside. And you always ate all of your vegetables; the veritable perfect child, or so it would seem."

"Damn you, jerk head," I am ready to scoot off, but I don't leave.

Paul's eyes harden. "Then I told her that you only began to fall apart when you began partying hard."

"And you didn't mention a certain event?"

He ignores my question. "I told Alicia that even when you were bombed out of your skull you had this obsessive-compulsive thing that drove Izzy and me crazy. Mac didn't like it much either, probably still doesn't."

My blood goes from simmer to boil; still I sit there waiting for the coup de grace.

Now Paul tilts his head, stares with tired eyes and pastes a crazy smile across his lips.

"You'd come home from a beach party, shit-faced and barely able to walk, but you'd still sit down and get the sand out of your shoes, hold them up and inspect them for a stray grain of sand! And then—" He breaks into hysterical laughter. "Then you would line them up neatly under your bed before passing out." He does his fake yachting laugh as I struggle out of my chair to hobble away. "Miss Perfection," he roars. "Au revoir, Mon Cherie!"

But then I circle back, leg throbbing, breathing fire.

He gets up to pull out my chair. "Sit down," he commands.

"Shut up," I say. Now it's my turn.

"Sometimes I wonder if we had the same parents—we're so different."

He lifts his coffee mug, "Vive le difference!" "Tell you what we're gonna do, Sophia. We'll hire some nice farm girls to stay with Mom. I'm going to put an ad in the *Belle Haven Gazette* and you can interview them, pick the ones that you want and train 'em."

"Never mind that I have a husband and a business to return to."

"There's no one else who can do this but you."

"What about Alicia?" I ask, calming down. "Isn't she a big shot in Human Resources and a good judge of character? I could have sworn that she wrote a book on training rank and file employees. Let's face it, Alicia fits the bill."

"Leave her out of this," he growls. I'm particularly interested in why he is so sensitive about Alicia. Ah, but in vino veritas—hmmm.

"Maybe Izzy can come," I say foolishly. For some reason this sets him off again.

"Girl, this might hurt but that's what we're all about sometime, hurting each other."

I brace myself again.

"You and Mac sit up there on PEI so far out in the boondocks that it automatically excuses you from family problems."

"Oh God, why do I bother to talk to you," I'm ready to leave now.

"Actually, I have big clients who pay $450 an hour to talk to me, but that's not the reason I can't handle this. I can't do it because who I would hire would be wrong according to you!"

"Whatever, I'm going to bed." I start to get up when Paul grabs my hands and sits me back down."

"Oh, now you're going to get violent?"

"No, now we are going to clear the air, just like Mom wants us to. We're long overdue."

"Fine, but I would prefer it if you were sober, Paul. The decks are uneven."

He's quiet, thinking. "I can't do this sober," he says, surprising the hell out of me.

His voice grows husky. "You blame me for the accident."

I shake my head, confused as to why he would think that.

"Of course I don't. That's ridiculous," I say, staring hard.

He closes his eyes. "You don't have to lie to me. I'm a big boy, I can take it."

"I'm not lying. Why would I blame *you*?"

"Because you do!" His eyes bore into mine. "We both know that if I hadn't yelled out to Jack on the trail he wouldn't have lost his concentration. He'd be alive today, you'd be married to him and I ruined that for you, Sophia. That, my girl, is why you hate me." He orders another drink as I sit flabbergasted.

"Oh my God, Paul, you didn't cause Jack to fall, it was that damn dog! Mac tried to warn him, but it was too late. The dog bumped into Jack and he must have stepped back instead of pressing himself into the mountain."

Paul opens his mouth and stares at me. "Don't play with my head. Soph."

"I'm not, it's true. That's exactly what happened."

"Tell me again," he demands, desperately trying to sober up.

I repeat myself and sit there watching my brother sink into his chair. He begins to cry, exploding into huge gulping sobs. He covers his eyes with one hand, reaches out for mine with the other.

"Then why do you hate me?" he whispers.

"I don't hate you. I just react to your nastiness, that's all. You're always so fresh-mouthed with me that I try to avoid you."

"Oh God!" he weeps.

"I love you for God's sake, you're my little brother."

"I love you, too, Soph. That's why I was there. I didn't

come to New Hampshire to see Jack. I came because I was losing my big sister to him. I came to be with you."

Somehow I find the strength to continue. "Then why didn't you come to the hospital when they locked me up?"

"Because I thought you wouldn't want to see me. Because I thought it was my fault."

"And all these years that you were too busy to come to PEI?"

"Because I never knew why you married Mac. And I didn't want to see you, knowing that you settled for Mac because of what I caused."

I leaned as close to my brother as I could, despite the alcoholic fumes from his breath.

"Mac is the best husband in the world! When I hit bottom, it was Mac who rescued me. Believe me, I got the better end of the deal. We came to terms about Jack a long time before we let ourselves fall in love, bro."

"Then why were you drinking for so many years?"

"Because I'm an alcoholic, that's why. Just like Mom, and I daresay, just like you."

"Come here," my little brother says, opening his arms. When I don't move fast enough he gets up and scoops me onto his lap. Then, just like when we were kids, he pulls my hair, tweaks my nose and wiggles his ears.

"It was the dog?" he asks, burying his face in my hair.

"Yes, Paul, the big black dog. It almost took me with him, Paul. Mac pulled me back in the knick of time."

When his sobbing returns, I nuzzle under his chin. "Mmm, you smell good," is all I can manage, realizing that it is the smell of his drink, not his aftershave that triggers the remark."

SIXTY-EIGHT

When I return to our room, Fiona is awake, just coming from the bathroom.

"I never thought one human being could pee so much," she says, getting back into bed.

"I'm sure it's normal, honey. Don't worry about it."

"I'm not worried, but I have to ask you something?"

"Shoot," I say, kicking off my shoe before lining it up under my side of the bed.

"Don't you think I look awfully big for being in my eighth month?" As she smoothes the top sheet over her belly, I have to admit she's pretty big.

"I've never been pregnant, Fi. I wouldn't know. Are you sure about your due date?" All of a sudden I have this horrific vision of her going into labor in the car, but I know God wouldn't do that to us.

"Not really. I stained a little before losing my period so there's an off chance that I could've already been pregnant. I don't know."

A little voice in my head sends an alarm. "Tell you what, let's get you to a doctor when we get back to Belle Haven, okay?"

"Yeah," she smiles, and then she notices that my eye makeup has streaked down my cheeks.

"Did you and Uncle Paul have a fight?" She sits up, pats the bed and Cupcake pulls his hefty body up next to her. The dog rests its head on Fiona's leg.

"A beauty, and then we made up big time," I say grinning. Suddenly I'm hungry as a bear, dying for something sweet. "I'm going to call room service and get some pie sent up. Want something?"

"Yeah, apple pie with a slice of cheddar and some vanilla ice cream would be great," she says. "Maybe I'll take Cupcake for a pee pee now so I can sleep a little more in the morning."

"No, let me. You call downstairs and give them the order. Then when I get back it'll be here."

"But you can't walk him with your leg like that."

"Watch me," I say, fastening his leash to his collar and heading for the door.

Cupcake and I slip through the lobby, past a gaggle of revelers. There's a nice patch of grass across the street and the dog is grateful to squat. With his body, I assume it's not possible for him to lift his leg.

"Good dog," I say, feeling foolish for praising an animal for taking a leak, but that's what I've always done with my own pets. Cupcake rewards my praise by circling around a new patch of grass and making a nice, firm poopie. I scoop it up in the plastic bag I've taken for this very purpose, look for a waste can and find none. So we return through the lobby and there, next to the elevator, a receptacle awaits my neat package.

Back in the room, our feast is ready. Mom is snoring, and Peekay has arched his body around the top of her head. Good.

"On the ride down here, you were in the middle of quite a story, Fi. Feel like continuing?"

Fiona studies my tired face. "Can you take it? I mean you seemed to get queasy and I totally understand. I just wanted someone in the family to know the real deal, that's all."

"I'm glad you chose me, baby, so give me the real deal."

***

Fiona takes a big forkful of pie, a bite of cheddar and a spoonful of ice cream, washes it down with a swig of milk, and then shifts around until she gets comfortable.

"I'm not going to tell you what I did during the six years I was a junkie. You can use your imagination. What I *will* tell you is how I happened to decide to stay clean."

"Great," I say unable to hide the relief I feel. I really don't want to hear the dirty details.

"You remember my dad, don't you?"

"Of course, he was a great guy, a gorgeous hunk, too. How old were you when he died?"

"Fifteen. You know that I went to live with Nana and Zaydie Bernstein, but Nana fell and Zaydie had a stroke, so they had to go live in that senior center when I was eighteen. That's when I figured it was time to rekindle the relationship with my mom. Even though she wasn't what you'd call the ideal mom, I loved her. Besides, being with her was always an adventure. Plus, her mom was Gran and you know how I feel about Gran."

I refilled my teacup, eager for her to continue.

"Anyway, I'd gone to visit Dizzy—"

I laugh at the foolish name she calls her mother because it fits her to a T.

"It was when she was living in Marin in the woods."

"Right."

"Now imagine this for a score. Dizzy's roommate, Inez, sold pharmaceuticals and the house and her car were loaded with samples! Anyway, I was on Spring break, which is really a lie because I'd dropped out of USC already; still, I celebrated

Spring break. Any excuse for a party. Actually, I was dead broke, hitchhiked home, embarrassed to tell Dizzy that I didn't have bus fare."

"What happened to the money your dad left you?" I remembered it was rumored to be over $100,000.

Fiona shakes her head. "I cracked up three cars, went to India and Greece, and then spent the rest partying—designer drugs, you name it."

I nod.

"Anyway, when I got to Dizzy's I had enough smack to last me a week so I was in pretty good shape. Besides, I knew how easy it would be to score in Mill Valley. I was a pro in every sense of the word." Fiona lets the statement hang there. I get it but don't acknowledge that I do. She waits, I don't react.

"So, what happened?" I urge her to continue.

"Dizzy was home when I got there. First thing she does is announce that she's gay again. Like, who cares? Believe it or not she was baking cookies for me, something she'd done maybe twice before during my entire childhood."

"That's sweet, though." I'm sorry that she's still so angry with my sister.

Sweet? Now these weren't chocolate chip cookies or anything that would cure the munchies; they were granola, oatmeal, raisin, sprout, kelp, crap that was tasteless and guaranteed to clean out your gut within hours of eating just one. Dizzy ate most of the batch and seemed perfectly fine, a term I use loosely when it comes to my mother.

Fiona finishes off the last mouthful of pie, while I pour myself another cup of tea.

"Inez came home that night after a business trip and Dizzy greeted her with a long, disgusting kiss. 'You know that I'm gay now', she says again in case I hadn't heard her before, or maybe she said it so Inez could hear her, I don't know. Like, duh. I could give a shit. No, I was much more interested in what Inez did for the big drug company and where she kept her samples. After all, that was the real reason for my visit."

"Ay. I see where this is going."

"Inez read my mind so easily that I actually liked her. She said, 'Let's get this out on the table, I know you party and that you think you've come to the mother lode, so let's put your mind at ease and have a great visit. I've locked up every sample of every drug along with your mother's and my prescription medication. We've left Advil and Maalox in the medicine cabinet, that's all.' So I turned to my mother and asked her if she was going to let Inez talk to me like that. Actually, I already knew the answer. Dizzy had never taken care of me in her life so why should she start now."

Fiona can do great imitations and this one's a beauty. 'It's for your own good, dear.' she mimics, sounding like an old rerun of Ozzie and Harriet." I laugh, although I feel a tightening in my chest.

"God, how I loved the challenge! Within twenty-four hours I found the keys to the locked cabinet and spare keys to Inez's car. I wasn't having such a good time anyway, so what the heck. I took Dizzy's gym bag, emptied the cabinet, then took Inez's Toyota and headed down to Mill Valley. I could sell the drugs for good dough, build up my own stash, buy a bus ticket and get outta town before they returned from their daily jog. This was a great plan, except Inez saw me going down the road and called the cops. She pressed charges and I found myself in a crummy jail cell in the richest county in America. Worse, I needed a fix very badly."

"I had no idea," I say, wondering why Izzy had kept this from me.

"When Dizzy and Inez came to see me I was sweating, shaking and clawing my itchy body. Inez was smart. She told me that she knew I rode the horse and Dizzy got insulted. She got very indignant and told Inez that I wasn't crazy. So I started screaming at Dizzy and said if she didn't get me out of there she'd never see me again. Then I said uglier things about how I got the money for drugs just to haunt her."

"So what happened then?" I ask, mesmerized that the tale being told is by and about a member of my family.

"Inez grabbed Dizzy's hand and they walked out the door, leaving me to the California system. No more bailing me out; no more lying to the family to cover for me; no more lying to herself. Dizzy grew balls."

I think about my sister and realize how much courage it must have taken for her to take those steps.

"I nearly died in detox. Then, when I was barely strong enough to walk, I had to go to court because Inez really did press charges. Yet somehow, maybe through Inez' connections because she sold psychotropic meds, I ended up on scholarship at a rehab facility in Boca. Not the glitzy side of Boca, no, this was in a strip mall surrounded by fruit stands and furniture stores. I laughed when I got there, but it's run by some of the toughest, smartest former junkies from New York City. Seriously, for someone as sick as I was it's probably the best place in this country."

I remember hearing about the place from Izzy, who assured all of us that this was the last stop on the road for Fiona.

"I found out that I'm bipolar so first they treated me for that. It's really tough getting the meds down right, and then treated me for my addiction."

"Amazing, Fi. I didn't know that you're bipolar. Thank God you went into treatment, you must've been ready."

"Hah. For the first five months I was just going through the motions because I didn't have anywhere else to go, no car, no money, and no friends who were straight. And I couldn't go back to Dizzy's, that was a given. I was a thief and until I completed my treatment I would never enter her home again."

"She did that because she loves you and was told to hang tough."

"I know that now, but I still hated her back then so to make her pay for my problems I would call her every few days, running up her phone bill just because it felt good. I'd tell her about the crazy people I was in treatment with, how I was in danger, that I hadn't eaten for days, and any other major lie I could think of just to make her feel guilty. And it worked! I know for a fact that she drove the staff crazy on the phone because once I heard my therapist say that my mother was a poster child for co-dependency."

"She did what she thought was right, Fi. Life's been hard on her, and maybe she was right, I mean, look at you now. You're healthy, you're sober—"

"And don't forget, pregnant. Anyway, in my fifth month of treatment my therapy team decided that I should work part-time. Some people had jobs at movie theatres, others worked at fruit stands and a few of the girls worked in a bookstore. Most of their families were shocked that their dear darling college grads would be asked to do menial labor. Tough noogies, you dig?"

"I dig. So where did you work, I didn't know you had a job?"

Fiona shifts, moves closer, eyes soft as butter. "I took care of crack babies. If you want to be scared straight, volunteer to do the work I did for even a day."

I nod, spellbound.

"It was run by the State for, you know, junkies. I worked there for six months, three days a week. My job was to just hold the babies, to give them human kindness, to speak softly to them, soothe them as they went through withdrawal and suffered from the actions of their mothers." Fiona rubs her belly and I look away, worried about the real state of her health.

"I sang to those babies and they'd stop crying; so I'd sing again and again until my throat was raw. Then one day, when it was 98 degrees out, my ride back to rehab was late. It was August and you could fry eggs on the street. I stood under a tree, pissed off and steaming until someone tugged my arm. It was Kadisha, one of the mothers of the crack babies who'd been there to see her little boy.

"She said, 'My baby loves you.' I don't remember exactly what I said, but I'm sure it showed that I pitied her. Funny thing, though, Kadisha didn't mind. She told me that I had a gift and just as the van pulled up she said she hoped that I'd use it. I remember getting into the van and there was some Salsa music blaring; Rodrigo was driving, grooving to the beat. He was so into the music I didn't have to talk with him and that was good, because I thought about what Kadisha had said until I got to my meeting that night. I was in a fog, barely listening to people share their thoughts, and then, Auntie Soph, I knew. Some people believe in God; others admit there's a Higher Power, and I'm somewhere in between. It came to me!

"I'd lived such a screwed up life, done some things that would make your hair curl. I've seen junkies die! Truthfully, I just wondered when my time would come. Suddenly, I wanted to live. I felt I had a purpose on this earth and it was time to accept it."

I cannot speak as my tears flow.

"Don't cry, Auntie. That's when the light went on in my head. I learned the rules and lived by them, but it took time. I was in rehab for fourteen months before I was sure I was ready to move into their halfway house. When my scholarship ran out, Uncle Paul picked up the rest of the tab that Social Security disability wouldn't cover. I took one day at a time and I realized that I wanted to live a full life. I wanted to *feel* again."

Fiona's smiling, looking happy and strong and I have withered to a sopping mess.

"You want to know when I had my first real thought that it would be all right? It was when I knew that I wanted to have sex to feel what *feeling* felt like, so I chose the nicest guy in our house, and we found a quiet spot where we could explore each other and make love. It felt good. Not great, just good, know what I mean?" I nod, of course I do.

"The shrinks said that I was sending a message to the world that I'm alive."

"So is he the baby's father?"

"No," she says then turns on the radio.

***

After saying good night I hear her weeping.

"What wrong, honey?"

"Nothing, the baby is doing a tap dance, that's all."

I'm sick at heart, knowing that she wants to keep her child but is afraid that she can't afford to keep a roof over their heads and food in their mouths. I suggest, "Maybe we can all chip in and help you get on your feet."

"No, this is God's plan and I accept it." She stops crying and soon I can tell she is asleep, leaving me alone with my thoughts.

I've always spouted off about illegitimate children, saying that adoption was the best answer for the child, and the mother. That was so damn shortsighted, so pompous-asinine of me. That was before Fiona. I find myself looking at her belly and watching the movements, wondering if it's a foot I see rippling across the surface. Then I remember Fiona's dance recitals and I imagine this little one is a dancer. All I know is that this is my flesh and blood and I don't want strangers raising our blood child. Jesus, what a hypocrite I am!

Once we get to Belle Haven, I'm going to talk to Izzy and Paul.

SIXTY-NINE

I'm buying a gun! Even though it's a glorious day, Mom has been singing *"The Rain in Spain"* in a cockney accent for two hours, over and over. Sometimes she switches to a Spanish accent, other times it's French. If this isn't maddening enough, when we make a pit stop she and Fiona do a swooping dance as they both sing off-tune, dipping around the gas station like dodo birds. Then, as if my patience has not worn thin enough, Mom pees her pants not five minutes after we drive away.

Later, Mom demands that we pull into a cheesy diner, The Cat's Meow—get it—and she gobbles the greasiest cheeseburger I've ever seen. She orders bacon on top, of course. Fiona thinks it's wonderful that Mom has such a great appetite. I have to slow her down and convince her to take small bites, which don't go over well.

"Mom, you could choke on your food." I make the mistake of taking her arm to as she's about to stuff a fistful of French fries into her mouth.

"Help me, help me, this woman is hurting me," she screams at the people at the next table. Fiona tries to calm her, unsuccessfully.

When the man and woman from the next booth approach us, Mom says, "Oh, you're so fat, you're going to blow up!" Immediately, they stop feeling concern for her.

Fiona diverts Mom's attention by stuffing her with a salad, a ritual that she's performed since she joined our traveling sideshow.

"Eat your leafy greens, Gran; they're good for your brain."

Mom opens wide, and then gags. Poor Fiona thinks that she can cure Mom.

***

A half hour after dinner, Mom's bowel decides to put on a show for us. We pull over, change her, clean her up and, tell her it is not a problem, but I admit I have had it. To make matters worse, or more absurd, she was singing "*White Christmas*" while we dealt with the "issue". Even Peekay is perplexed. I plan to forget that he got loose during this, but we found him and locked him in his cage. Cupcake puts everything in perspective. When we get Mom back in the car, he waddles over to her, plomps down, puts his head in her lap and kisses her trembling hands. At this moment, I love that fleabag.

SEVENTY

As Fiona drives and Mom snoozes, I sink into a fugue state, remembering how Mac had argued with me when I told him that I wanted to live alone after the accident. I knew that he could have easily found roommates to fill the spaces left empty by Jack and me, but he wouldn't hear of it. "You are not living alone," he had dictated, ignoring the fact that I was heavily drugged on Valium and could barely speak my name. Still, I had tried.

"Do it for Jack," Mac had bargained. So I went back to class despite Izzy's invitation to live with her in San Francisco. It was the wrong decision—for Mac and for me.

The MacDougals live like Ozzie and Harriet in Bangor, Maine. His family is quite sane; they hold down good jobs, pay their bills on time and go to church. They have family reunions, write long letters to enclose with Christmas cards and are polite to a point of being boring. Randy MacDougal owned an insurance agency before he retired; his wife Catherine still gives piano lessons in her fern-filled living room. They eat franks and beans on Saturday nights and were active in the P.T.A. while Mac was growing up.

Mac was the good kid in the neighborhood. He was the one who shoveled snow for old widows without taking a dime. He was an Eagle Scout and got his picture in the *Bangor News* when he came in third in the Soap Box Derby driving a plywood car he'd built by himself. He sailed through Bangor

High School, a strong a student, student council member, and a great athlete. He had his choice of many colleges, and chose Michigan because he liked the hockey coach who had recruited him.

In his high school senior year, he started going steady with Nancy Hopkins, captain of the cheerleading squad, who was headed for the University of Maine, Oromo, just seven miles from Bangor. It was assumed that they would marry some day, if the distance didn't drive them apart. Their plans ended the day of Jack's accident, although Mac didn't end it until he went home for that Thanksgiving. Mac being Mac, he wanted to break it off in person.

I had tried to pick up my life after the accident and maybe I would have succeeded had it not been for my growing dependence on alcohol to relieve my pain. Even though I loved to drink before the accident, I always waited until the weekend before getting trashed. After the accident, I started drinking a few beers every night after dinner. Then I drank a few beers *instead* of dinner. Needless to say, it was impossible for me to concentrate on my studies, so when my advisor suggested I take the rest of the semester off, I was relieved. And I was furious.

My family and Mac had dragged me back into the life of the living, believing in clichés and not recognizing the depth of my despair. I was desperately in need of counseling but refused to go. Instead, I chose booze and pot, a great mixture if you want to fry your brain. Then, when the pain wouldn't subside, I started with pills—any pills, uppers, downers, anything I could get my hands on. Mac would come home from class to find me passed out, and he would sober me up. This became our routine until the day Mac came home to find me drunk and naked, in bed with a stranger. That's when he called my parents to come get me. And dare I say that's when Mac first realized that his feelings for me were more than friendship. After my father had picked me up in Ann Arbor, he drove me to a hospital in Minnesota, where I stayed for several months, fluctuating between wanting to die and trying to live.

SEVENTY-ONE

When he learned that I could finally have visitors, Mac left Bangor the day after Christmas to be able to visit with me on New Year's Eve. He drove through a blizzard, went off the road twice, but fought his way to Minnesota just so he could surprise me for New Year's Eve. I remember how down I was that afternoon, feeling sorry for myself as I ate my holiday turkey dinner. Some of the patients had received special passes to spend the evening with their families at local hotels, but my family had come for Christmas, so I was alone.

When Mac found me in the television room he looked like a scared rabbit. He held a bouquet of red roses in one hand and a bag of presents for me in the other. The staff had known that he was coming and had cut back on my meds so I would be lucid enough to communicate with him. With a therapist standing nearby, Mac called out my name. It sounded like someone calling through a tunnel. Mac said that when I saw him I smiled the saddest smile he'd ever seen. When he reached my side, he dropped to his knees so I could look down on him, thinking that it would give me a feeling of being in control. Sweet, sensitive Mac.

An orderly brought a vase for the roses and set them on the table in front of us. My motor skills were not good enough to untie ribbons so Mac opened his gifts for me. His mother had knitted an angora scarf in a beautiful shade of rose; his father had wrapped a calendar that featured beautiful Maine landscapes and the name of his insurance agency. Mac had chosen a teddy bear as my gift. It was small enough to sit on the table next to my bed, and large enough to cuddle. The bear wore a red ribbon with a heart dangling from it. Months later, when I was packing it in my suitcase I saw that the heart had been engraved. It read, "S.I.L.Y., Mac".

"What does it stand for," I'd asked him when he came to the lake a few months later.

"I can't tell you just yet," he'd answered.

It took two more years, a "refresher" month in rehab, and thousands of AA meetings for me to find the meaning of S.I.L.Y.

When Mac graduated from Michigan he was hired by a major accounting firm to work in their Chicago office. We caught up with each other pretty often, for baseball games, concerts or sometimes just to be together. He had a nice apartment with a view of Lake Michigan and I liked being there with him. When he suggested that we spend Thanksgiving together in Belle Haven and then head back to Chicago for Christmas shopping, I thought it was a great idea. I looked forward to seeing the decorations in the storefronts and the blazing lights along the shore. I should have known something was up when easygoing Mac's hands began shaking during dinner that Saturday night. Cleverly, Mac had smuggled a package under his coat and after we finished eating he brought it out and handed it to me. It was another teddy bear, same color, same ribbon, same heart, but this time it read, 'Sophia, I Love You. Marry me, Mac. I was stunned, and yet I wasn't. I was speechless and then I rattled on for five minutes about the food, the lights, the shopping, until finally I reached across the table to hold his trembling hands and told him that I'd be honored to be his wife.

We went back to his apartment to seal the deal in the biblical sense. Our lovemaking was glorious, a celebration of life, of friendship, and now a lifetime commitment to one another.

Before slipping a beautiful engagement ring on my finger, Mac told me that he wanted to move to Canada. His uncle had died and left him a few hundred acres of land near the ocean.

"Everything will be fresh and new," he had promised.

It was. It still is.

SEVENTY-TWO

Today, I'm furious that we live in Canada, and that we aren't rich, and that we didn't spend more time with my mother. I'm just damn mad.

Mac says the bakery orders are coming in fast. He can spell me for another week, and then I have to get back to the Island to take care of the biggest month of the year. After that, I might be able to return to Wisconsin for awhile. I'm scared, but before I can dwell on it, Fiona asks to use my laptop.

To: PVorelli@lawfrm.com
          IsabelaCam-aok@hotmail.com
From: Sophia@peisland.net
Subject: It's me, Fiona, using Aunt Sophia's email

Hi Uncle Paul, Hi Dizzy:

I know that you all have issues with me and that they are more than justified, but I have a potential solution to our family situation. I would be willing to quit my job and move in with Gran if I could be paid what you would ordinarily pay a housekeeper. I called my sponsor last night and she checked on NA and AA groups. There are two meetings I can choose from in Belle Haven and she thinks I could handle it as long as I could get relief from a home health aide two days a week.

Luckily, the drugs didn't burn out all of my brain cells and I've been using Aunt Sophie's laptop to do a lot of research about Alzheimer's. I know that Gran could be difficult to handle, but I'd like to give it a try. I'm not holding out for any miracles—I know she is on her way to join our God, but I'd rather have her in the care of someone who loves her as much as I do. What do you think?

Love
Fiona

To: Sophia@peisland.net
        PVorelli@lawfrm.com
From: IsabelaCam-aok@hotmail.com
Subject: Fiona

Sophia—please share this with my daughter.

Dearest Fiona:

When I read your email I began to cry. I kept asking myself what I have done to deserve such a loving, caring daughter. Afterwards, you may find this hard to believe, I went to an NA meeting. Long overdue, but never too late, they tell me.

I went to the meeting hoping that someone would give me a good reason to tell you not to stay with Mom, but that didn't happen. What I heard was "one day at a time". What I also heard was that no one has the power to make decisions for another. That's the hard part for me.

I know that I failed you miserably while you were growing up. I hurt your father—the best man I've ever known—and I hurt my baby girl. It's no surprise that I've botched up my life pretty badly, but this isn't about me—it's about you, my sweet Fiona. Here's the bottom line: the stress of taking care of an Alzheimer's patient is unbelievable. You could only do it with a great deal of support, and honey, I can't give it to you, as much as I want to. I live in California, don't have an extra dime to speak of, and this time I don't want to make a promise to you which I can't keep. Uncle Paul is going to be in charge of what little money your grandmother has—and we'll have to wait and see if he thinks there's enough to pay a home health aide—and for how long.

What I want to say is this, baby. If you want to come to California I will take care of you and your baby. If I have to work three jobs, I'll do it, and since I plan to go to NA meetings, it's a promise I can keep today. I don't know about tomorrow. I'm just sick of failing you and I don't want to set you up for disappointment again.

Whatever you choose to do, know that I love you and will help you however I can.

Always my love,
Mama

Fiona is so grateful to get this message from her mother that she can't stop weeping. I am certain that she wants to keep the baby. She cradles her belly as only a pregnant woman can, guarding it as she moves around, rubbing it softly. Sometimes I catch her talking to her belly, and then she pulls Cupcake's ugly face to her and tells the dog that its baby brother or sister is in there.

Paul has done the math and it looks grim. We will be looking at about $400 a week for a live-in homemaker to care for Mom. She has enough money in her savings to last for about six months. After that, she may have to go into a nursing home. As for having Fiona take care of her, Paul agrees, provided someone could check up on Fiona regularly—someone like Nelly. He says we've got to put our faith back in Fiona and I agree. He doesn't want to give her check-signing privileges, but he can arrange to pay for bills from his office.

I'm concerned about back-up for Fiona, as well as her own state of health. Big, pregnant women need their rest. I wouldn't want to see her running down the street after Mom, go into labor, and lose all of them. Furthermore, if Mom has to go to a nursing home we will have to sell the house and that would leave Fiona with nowhere to live, so Paul thinks we'd have to make some financial arrangements in advance to cover that.

It's complicated but thank you, Jesus. I'm feeling a little better.

SEVENTY-THREE

To: PVorelli@lawfrm.com

         IsabelaCam-aok@hotmail.com

From: Sophia@peisland.net

Subject: Kentucky Rain

This letter is being dictated by our mother to all of us. I am correcting her English and filling in the missing words, but don't be fooled, she is failing. Still, I think she understands the issue.

Sophia

LAMBS:

The Kentucky rain washed away the cobwebs. This is what I want.

No strangers in my house! (She repeats this over and over). No big fat country girl eating pie and all that goo—on my money. Nelly's sister had a fat farm girl who broke the toilet and fell through the floor. (Mom laughs hysterically at this.)

Fiona will live with me. (She pounds her fist). Her and my itty bitty baby. No one can take her baby away.

Love,

Mom

Paul calls the minute he reads my email.

"I vote for Fiona."

"Me, too."

"Izzy will too."

"Then it's settled."

"Yes, it is, and guess what? The case is over and I'm coming to Wisconsin. I'll be there by the time you get there."

"Oh, Paw-Paw, thank you." Huh? Well, who am I to argue. I'm over the moon.

"Don't thank me, hon. You're the hero here."

A lump forms in my throat.

"I've started contacting agencies so we can interview home health aides who can relieve Fiona."

I sigh then, the tears come.

"Listen, Soph. I can't talk anymore but why don't you check your email."

When I hang up I remember that his case is supposed to continue for two more weeks. God, I hope I didn't put him on such a guilt trip that he's blown it, so I call his office and they tell me he isn't there. He's at home, they say. I call the house but he doesn't answer. Now I'm worried. Why is the hair on my arm standing up like it was the time I couldn't find him at a rock concert and he had been busted? I think I'll check my email.

To: Sophia@peisland.net

        IsabelaCam-aok@hotmail.com

From: LawlessOne@hotmail.com

Subject: It's me, Paul

Girls: This is my private, personal email account that I just set up last night. Let's get this out of the way. I lost the case and my firm is insisting that I take a leave of absence so I can get some rest and put my life back together. I've worked eighteen-hour days, seven days a week for so long that I can't imagine what I will do without my crazed schedule. As soon as we arrange things in Wisconsin, I'm going down to a beach shack I've rented in Tortola where I am hoping that I'll be able to hear myself think. I'm know I'll be able to count on your strength if I need help.

Alicia and I have been separated for three months because she didn't see the point of having an absentee husband. Working at the office on Christmas was the last straw, she said. The kids are disgusted with me and they think the way I've shoved my head in the sand over Mom is indicative of what a cold, unfeeling bastard I am. I spent all day yesterday walking in the woods, thinking about Mom and about our family. I'm not sure how long I cried, but it seemed like forever. Even now, as I write this to you, tears are streaming down my stubbly cheeks. I just can't stand the thought of watching her turn into a vegetable. I just hope and pray that we can work this out in a way that makes all of us feel comfortable, most importantly, Mom.

I'm sorry for all the years of mouthing off, Soph, and for shutting you out, Izzy. I love you both. I just want

to curl up on Mom's lap and have her tell me that this has all been the work of the boogiemen.
See you soon,
Paul

PS Sophia, before she is completely out of it, can you get the garlic chicken recipe?

To: LawlessOne@hotmail.com
         IsabelaCam-aok@hotmail.com
From: Sophia@peisland.net
Subject: You

Dearest, dearest Paul,

Your email has touched me more than you can ever imagine. Although I'm sorry you lost your case, I'm glad that you are coming to your senses about being a workaholic and the sacrifices you've made. For so many years I've wished that you and I would be close again. But after Louisville, I'd say we've made a great start.

There's something I need to tell you, Paul, because if we're clearing the air, you have a right to know that the cold air between us blew in both directions. While I was tearing you down for cheating on Alicia, it was my own guilt that made me so angry.
Five years ago, I fell off the wagon and the ever-patient Mac left me for six months while I sobered up. To punish him, I had an affair in rehab and made sure Mac found out about it. But we found our way

back to each other and our loving is honest and easy once more. I pray the same will happen for you and Alicia, too.

Sometimes I lie awake at night and think that God is punishing Mom because of what I've done and it makes me so sick I want to run away. Other times, I just lie there, wishing I could take care of her and then these terrible scenarios run through my mind and I know I can't do it. I mean, I know I won't do it. Does this make me evil? I don't know, Paw-Paw, does it?

Just know this, bro. You were always my hero and you always will be. I know how you tried to save Jack and how much you suffered after the accident. I will never forget how you cradled his bloody head and tried to revive him. I remember how you were trying to hold his skull together until the rangers pulled you away. And I remember beating you with my fists and you just stood there and took it. But until Louisville, I never understood why. Oh, to take back those wasted years, honey. God, how I've missed you.

Just know this, my little brother. I'm here for you and we'll get Izzy on the horn and figure things out.

Much love always,
Sophia

Izzy is ecstatic. "Hot damn! All I can say is AWESOME. The two of you are AWESOME—I can't believe I'm related to you. Listen, I know I've been a pain in the butt with the high drama of my life, and I know you don't take me too seriously, but here goes anyway. Mahatma and I were married in a commitment ceremony in Hawaii last summer. She is a wonderful woman, very spiritual and kind, but there's a fly in the ointment. I've fallen in love with a wonderful *man* who's in my yoga class. Now talk among yourselves."

Click.

BELLE HAVEN, WISCONSIN

SEVENTY-FOUR

I STILL CAN'T BELIEVE IT!!! Peekay is the hero of our family! Who ever thought I'd say that? There I was, unpacking Mom's suitcase, and Peekay was on the bed playing with Mom's wicker and wood purse. He kept trying to bat open one of the lids, but his claw kept getting stuck in the wicker. I shooed him away, but he was persistent. I figured there was a tasty morsel in there that Mom hadn't remembered to feed him. Finally, he got his claw stuck again, yanked too hard and he and the purse went tumbling to the floor. When he broke free, he yowled and ran off.

I picked up the purse and turned it upside down to shake out the remaining hamburger bits. Then, in slow motion—a $200 ticket from the Kentucky Derby floated to the floor. Where in hell did Mom get $200? It took me a few minutes to believe that in my trembling hand I held the answer to our problems. I checked the ticket one more time and yes, it read Prince Karl's Passion. Two hundred dollars on the winner—the long shot! Mamma mia.

"Fiona, come here quick!" I show her the ticket and her jaw drops.

"So that's what Gran did when she took off."

"Bingo, Fiona. She placed her bet, and then forgot about it. When the horse she bet on with you lost, that was the end of it."

"Where on earth did she get $200?"

I think for a moment. "She could have had a stash somewhere set aside for this moment in her life, or who knows? Do I care? Absolutely not."

Fiona keeps her cool and calls Churchill Downs. All we have to do is mail in the ticket and they'll send back a check. Since the horse was a long shot, Mom's $200 winning ticket is worth $132,224!

"You won, Mom, you're rich!" I hug and kiss her, hoping that she understands what has happened.

"Of course I won. I know how to pick 'em." Her eyes twinkle for a moment.

"Why did you bet on Prince Karl's Passion?" She looks at the ticket for a long time, then points to the "P" and the "K".

"Peekay—Prince Karl—PEE KAY! Got it?"

"Stupid me, I should have figured that out, Gran," Fiona says, curling up next to her. I hobble to my pocketbook. Without thinking twice, I open my wallet and pull out my emergency American Express card. I hand it to my niece.

"Fiona, here's my credit card. Buy that cat a new collar and a slab of salmon while you're at it. I'll call the butcher and order a big filet roast for dinner. Paul will be here any minute and it's his favorite meal."

"Fiona looks at my Amex card, and then looks at me. Her nose crinkles and she swallows hard. "Thank you for trusting me again."

I realize how far we've come on our journey. It seems to me that God always has a plan.

SEVENTY-FIVE

The garlic infused roast smells like heaven as it cooks in Mom's well-seasoned oven. I think about the many roast beefs and turkeys we've pulled from the racks of her Hotpoint and I find myself smiling at the stove.

Cupcake is being given a lapping bath by Peekay the Savior. Suddenly, my childhood home is ours once more. It won't take too much work to make it sparkle again. Maybe we'll paint the living room in a warm butter yellow. Mom loves that color.

"How about warm coral for the dining room?" Fiona calls from the dining room."

"And we'll make the nursery into a fairy tale," I tell my niece. "I can paint doggies on the walls if you want me to."

"Oh Auntie," she says throwing her slender arms around my neck. She smells of her Gran's Shalimar and I think it's the most wonderful scent in the world.

**

Fiona is singing another Elvis song while she sets the table. It's *"The Wonder of You"* and my heart stops short. Whenever Jack sang that song, no matter where he was, he would look only at me and I would melt away. But that was then, and this is now.

I hear Paul's footsteps on the front porch and clomp out to greet him. He looks tired and beat, a little disheveled and sheepish, but to me he looks better than Robert Redford did in "The Way We Were," and that's as good as it gets. He puts down his suitcase, gathers me up and swings me around. Then my brother smiles that winning smile which shows off the deepest dimples east of the Pacific and cups my face in his hands.

He bends down so we are eyeball to eyeball, a question forming on his lips.

"So Soph, did you get the garlic chicken recipe?"

I roll my eyes before I burst out laughing. "Why don't you ask Mom for it," I answer, finally winning a round.

Much later that evening, after we've stuffed ourselves with a wonderful meal and great stories of our trip, Paul has a chance to feel Fiona's baby kick.

"That's a Heissman Trophy winner," he says, so sure of himself as usual. I leave him with Fiona as I get Mom in her striped Lanz nightgown, then sit with her while she nurses a mug of cocoa.

"I love you, Mom," I say, planting a goodnight kiss on her cheek.

"You too," she says. Then, very seriously she asks, "Who's that good-looking man?"

"That's your son, Paul,"

"Oh," she says, and then ponders a thought. "I did good, didn't I?" obviously proud of her handsome son.

"Mom, you did great!"

When I'm sure Mom's asleep I leave her bedroom to rejoin the others. A storm's been blowing for the last hour, rattling the windows and tossing around unraked leaves from the fall.

Fiona's cleaning up in the kitchen while Paul spreads Mom's bills and bank statements across the dining room table.

"Need any help?" I call to the kitchen.

"No, I'm all finished," Fiona says, bringing me a warm cup of cocoa. She's such a wonderful girl. I just hope and pray that she'll meet a man who'll love her and want to be a father for her child.

***

Paul has disappeared. I find him in the den looking at the window on the east side of the house. He's a million miles away

"A penny for your thoughts, bro."

He stands straight, rocking back on his heels, his hands shoved deeply into the pockets of his Dockers.

"I was just remembering the summer that Jimmy Burke and I darkened most of the town with our b-b guns."

"Yeah, you were great shots, although it was hard to miss the huge streetlights. How long were you grounded for?"

"Four weeks, with hard labor and no ice cream."

"Didn't you get your mouth washed out with soap on the first day you were grounded?" I can remember him spouting off under his breath when he saw us in our bathing suits ready to go to the beach.

Paul laughs. "Hard labor meant digging up a big expanse of the side lawn so Mom could plant a shade garden. She asked me to help her drag the Adirondack chair over to where I was working."

"God, I remember that chair." It was always her favorite chair, painted dark, hunter green. The arms were wide enough to hold her big fat book on plants."

"Anyway, after I dragged over the chair she set up her easel and filled her jelly jar with water for her watercolors. As I dug up the lawn, turned it over, added peat moss and manure, Mom sketched out her shade garden."

"That sounds like Mom." I smile at Paul who still stands staring out the window, not looking at me.

"When she finished, she showed me her painting. Now I realize how clever she was. Her entire garden would be different shades of green, with plants that would bear only white blossoms. At first I thought it was dumb, no colorful flowers, nothing yellow or pink like the roses on the porch side. Then, as the weeks wore on, I understood her vision. It would be subtle and very stylish. Pure Mom."

Paul's voice is changing. He sounds younger as he talks, almost boyish. It's a story he needs to hear himself tell. I touch his shoulder, rub it gently. His arm circles my waist.

"Each day she taught me the Latin names of all the plants that I planted as she sat in that chair. And each day I grew to know her better. She read poetry aloud, and then explained what the verses meant to her, and then she asked what they meant to me."

"Oh Paw-Paw, she is so special and she loves you so much, honey. You've got that to remember for the rest of your life."

His eyes are filled with tears. He wears a look of disbelief, realizing that the Mom he describes has left us never to return. Together, we look at the garden barely illuminated by the den light.

"Every day while you guys were at the beach, Mom and I planted dozens of variegated hosta, lilies of the valley, Boston fern, white hydrangeas and rhododendron." Paul points to the plants, now overgrown and badly in need of a good weeding and pruning. When it was too hot to work, she'd fill the blue pitcher with the rabbit on it with lemonade. Then we would sit on the grass under the Colorado spruce and she'd tell me about her childhood."

"I remember when you and Mom finished the garden because you got all itchy from the pine bark mulch.

"I don't remember that, but I do remember what we did when we were finished."

"What?" I ask, feeling closer to my brother than I had in years.

"Mom and I walked to town where we sat at Crawley's soda fountain and celebrated with huge banana splits. As we walked home she pronounced me "ungrounded. Frankly, I was probably never more 'grounded' as I was that summer."

Paul's shoulders shake, his face is dark and pained. We hold each other closely, finding comfort in each other's arms.

SEVENTY-SIX

At first I think it's a branch slapping at the windowpane, until clearly there's a distinct tap on the living room window. It startles us and Paul charges past me to look outside. He presses his face against the window as we hear another tap.

"Who is that masked man?" he asks, suppressing a laugh as I hobble behind him.

It's amazing, but in the darkness I barely recognize the six-footer wearing a familiar jacket and a surgical mask.

"Mac! Oh my God." I start to open the window when he gestures for me to close it.

"I'm already wheezing," he explains through the mask. "Get your coat and meet me on the porch," he calls through the window.

I grab my coat and hobble to him, lifting his mask so I can taste his warm kiss.

"What are you doing here?" As if I need a reason for him to hold me in his arms.

"I just came by to tell you that I have a room at the Bramble Inn and I wonder if you'd like to shack up with me." He nuzzles my cheek and pats my butt.

My heart pounds with the fervor of a sixteen-year-old planning to sneak off for some serious necking. I can't believe Mac has done this. He always tells me that he hates to surprise people or to be surprised. Still, he's pulled off the surprise of the year and I love him for it.

I study his wonderful face and realize that he's waiting for a response.

"You must be joking," is all I manage to say.

"Oh I'm not joking," he answers, "I'm as serious as a rooster in a hen house." As he shakes his head his thick gray hair catches the moonlight. For a second, and because I've read far too many romance novels, he reminds me of a knight in shining armor.

"I can't believe this," I say as I call to Paul and Fiona that I'm off for the night.

Later, after we've greeted each other properly, he rubs my shoulders and my back, expertly massaging away the month.

"Has Duane St. George been by?" he asks, sounding like a nervous teenager.

"Oh my God, you're jealous!" I am bursting with delight. Imagine, after all these years! But Mac isn't smiling; he's dead serious.

"Well, Chiquita, let's just say that I'm sure you need to stay with your Mom a little longer and I thought I'd drop by to remind you what you have waiting for you on PEI."

Like I'd ever forget.

To round out our family's penchant for surprise visits, Izzy arrives the next afternoon. I haven't seen her for a few years, so I marvel at how fantastic she still looks. Her hair has turned that gorgeous shade of white that makes women wonder why they color their hair; her eyes are clear and sparkling and her posture is tall and proud. As happy as we are to see her, it brings special joy to Fiona.

"I'm glad you're here Dizzy," Fiona says. "I've been praying for you to come, but this is a sober house, so no pot or booze, okay?"

KENTUCKY RAIN

This last remark makes Izzy crumble. She hands me the bouquet of flowers she's brought, offers her cheek to me and Paul, and then maneuvers around her daughter's bulging belly to hold her in her arms and sobs so hard that we all join in.

Mom appears in her bedroom doorway. She's a sight with freshly applied lipstick that outlines much fuller lips than she's ever had. I'm sorry, I can't suppress a laugh.

"What's this rocket in my house? The rat can't sleep."

I look at Paul while Fiona translates. "She means racket and cat, don't worry; I always know what she means."

Izzy smiles, finally releasing her grip on Fiona. "Wow, we must be really loud if she can hear us." Izzy can't disguise the look of sadness on her face as she walks toward Mom.

"You're Isadora?" Mom asks.

"Close. I'm Isabella. Your long lost daughter's here, Mom," Izzy says as a tear slides down her cheek.

"You were lost?" Mom raises her voice and adds, "me too. Don't feel bad, Darlin, I'm lost all the time."

We share a good laugh while Fiona leads Mom back to bed.

***

Seconds later, we hear a loud thump coming from Mom's bedroom. We race in just as Fiona is lifting Mom into bed.

"Fiona, no," Izzy warns. "You'll hurt yourself."

"Calm down, Dizzy, I'll just lie here with her for awhile." Fiona shoos us out of the bedroom, directing me to close the door.

Izzy brews a pot of tea and puts forth a batch of "healthy" cookies, which Mahatma has baked for us. I take a polite bite, gag on the bran and God knows what else, but then I fish out the dates and nuts, smacking my lips for my sister's benefit. Paul gobbles two and reaches for a third.

"Save some for Fiona," Izzy says. Not a problem for me.

Paul grabs the television remote and suddenly we're kids again, fighting over what we'll watch. We settle on a "Seinfeld" rerun—the one with the golf ball that gets stuck in the blowhole of a whale. Mac is so full of Benadryl that he's out cold in the chair. The volume is rather loud so maybe she called out and we didn't hear her.

"Where's Fi?" Izzy asks during a commercial.

"She probably fell asleep with Mom. They did that a lot on the trip."

Izzy's internal alarm goes off. "Uh, uh," she says as she gets up to check on her daughter.

"Sophia!" Izzy screams from the bedroom. "Quick!"

SEVENTY-SEVEN

Paul and I crash into each other as we run to Mom's room. We find Mom squatting in the corner; her eyes focused on Fiona, who is also in a squat. She is in hard labor, panting and breathing, with Mom as her coach. Izzy is on her knees assessing the situation. Izzy holds her wristwatch in front of her face and places a hand on Fiona's belly. "Tell me when your next pain starts," she says. Fiona nods, and then scrunches up her mouth, "Now," she gasps.

"Let's get her on the bed," Paul says trying to sound calm.

"No," Mom cries. "This is how the Indians do it. They put gravy to work."

"She means gravity," Fiona says nearly losing her breath as her belly turns harder with a strong spasm.

"That's two minutes from the last one," Izzy says. She runs to the bathroom, and then returns with a clean white towel to spread underneath Fiona.

"Call 911," Izzy yells.

"No, Mom, I want to give birth here," Fiona cries. The use of the word "mom" stops Izzy in her tracks.

Just then Fiona lets out an ungodly scream, followed by a series of grunts.

I get down on the floor to peer between her legs, amazed at what I see.

"The heads out," I cry. "Okay Fiona, you can do it, honey."

A huge smile covers Mom's face, made even more evident by her lipstick. "Just like grandpa after mum went over the Gap with Daniel Goone," Mom clucks. No one corrects her.

Paul calls 9-1-1 and they're on their way.

Izzy is nearly hyperventilating. "If I could take all this pain for you I would, honey."

"Just let me squeeze your hand, Mom," Fiona pants.

Then with a huge push and growl as loud as a lioness, Fiona delivers a breathtakingly beautiful baby girl into her grandmother's waiting hands.

"Free at last!" Mom yells.

"Have my mother cut the cord," Fiona whispers, exhausted and weeping.

So that's what Izzy does, she cut the cord, and newly-arrived Chief Halvorsen instructs her how to tie it off.

I wrap the baby in a towel and place her in Mom's arms just as the EMT's arrive. Mom holds her ever so gently, counts her fingers and toes, forgets what comes after eight, and then plants a welcoming kiss on the infant's forehead.

"What's her name?" Halvorsen asks, as the EMT's lift Fiona onto a stretcher.

"I'm not sure," Fiona whispers, sounding weary and happy at the same time.

"Coretta," Mom answers. "Martin would love it."

Fiona brightens. "That's a beautiful name, Gran. That's what we'll call her."

"Will she have a middle name?" I ask as the EMT places little Coretta in Fiona's arms.

Fiona smiles brilliantly. "What do you think?" she answers, looking in the direction of her mother.

"Rose," Izzy announces. "Coretta Rose."

Mac appears in the doorway, groggy and masked, with both hands outstretched.

"What the hell is going on here?" he asks, confused until I put his grand-niece in his arms.

"Gitchy-goo," he says sounding like a cute dope. "What a nutty family you've just come into, you little doll."

Then, as if the day hadn't been crazy enough, the paramedic says to Mac, "I'll take her now, if that's okay, doc."

"Fine with me," Mac wheezes.

"Me, too," Mom says, her eyes never leaving the tiny bundle that promises another generation of Campbell women.

As they say, life goes on.

EPILOGUE

om was able to stay in her Belle Haven home for another full year, cared for by Fiona and two skinny farm girls who helped out around the clock. Mom called little Coretta "Rosebud", spending hours making funny faces at the little one while Cupcake and Peekay stood guard at the crib. Izzy stayed on for a month, fixing up the house and mending her relationship with her daughter. After tuning out on Tortola, Paul decided to give up the practice of law and turn to teaching. He and Alicia never reconciled, but he enjoys a much stronger and healthier relationship with his children.

As much as we didn't want to put Mom in a nursing home, it finally became unsafe for her to stay in her home, even with round-the-clock care. She had stopped sleeping and was up almost 24 hours a day, restless and agitated some of the time. After a few scares, including leaving gas burners on and drinking a bottle of shampoo, we made a painful decision. Despite Fiona's pleading and begging to keep Mom at home with her and Corey Rose, she finally agreed that the time had come. After careful investigation and with a great deal of effort, we found a place that specializes in care for Alzheimer's patients. Paul checked it out in person twice, once planned, once a surprise—and the place was special and right for Mom.

On a sunny Sunday morning, I took my last road trip with Mom.

I slowed down as we passed the swans, wanting the trip to take forever.

She's with Papa now. And that is good because as mother always loved to quote from an old Yiddish proverb...

Even in Paradise, it is not good to be alone.

The End

Charlotte Jerace holds a M.Ed. from Antioch University and worked as a partner in an international benefits consulting firm. She has received international recognition for her writing including several Telly Awards, a New York Film Festival Award, and the Gold Quill from the International Association of Business Communicators. Her short story, "Cannibals" was published by Provincetown Arts Magazine. In the area of nonfiction, her *Facing the Future* was published by Penguin Books. Her first children's book will be published in 2007. An avid gardener and beachwalker, Jerace is married with a family and divides her time between Cape Cod and Florida.

Made in the USA
Lexington, KY
18 March 2011